Sisters in Love

Women's Club Editions

Sisters in Love

❦

A Novel by

Henriette Hampton Morris

Summerhouse   Columbia, South Carolina

This is a work of fiction with imagined
characters and incidents.
But there were people like these in
a place like this during the time of the story.

Published in Columbia, South Carolina
by Summerhouse Press

Summerhouse Press
P.O. Box 1492
Columbia, SC 29202
(803) 779-0870
(803) 779-9336 fax
www.summerhousepress.com

Library of Congress Cataloging in Publication Data

FIRST EDITION

10 9 8 7 6 5 4 3 2 1

This book was written in memory of my
grandmother and her daughers.

It is for their daughters and sons also . . .

and for all the daughters and sons
yet to come.

I want to acknowledge the people without
whom this manuscript would have languished
on a closet shelf.

Thank you Ben and Dargan.
Also my thanks to Tracy Devine
and Robin Asbury.

Sisters in Love

❦

She almost sees his face. A few more moments of being very still and she will have it—the golden head topping the others on the crowded porch, white teeth against sunburned skin. She remembers the feel of her heart beating hard and fast. Ah, yes, she almost sees his face—his eyes, those blue eyes—

"Now, now, do let's wake up."

The nurse's loud voice obliterates the pictures forming in her mind's eye.

"Just look who's here!"

She feels such frustration she almost weeps, but, slowly she opens her eyes and blinks in the too bright sunlight.

"It's your son, your son!"

My son? Ridiculous. That's my father. The

shape of the head, the dark hair, the purposeful look—all Papa.

"Don't you recognize your son?"

Really, the woman's voice just grates.

Reluctantly, she concentrates on what is being said.

She knows her son, she loves him, she's proud of him, but she's too tired for all that now. It's all behind her, all of it. Why can't they understand that she's finished with the present? It's the past that interests her. She wants to be left in peace.

"Well," the harsh-voiced nurse says, "it's just not a good day. It's too bad, Doctor. Some days your mother is as bright as can be."

"Never mind." His voice is quiet.

Not like Papa there, more Mama. Yes, the voice and sweetness are very like Mama's.

She makes a big effort and opens her eyes and smiles at him.

"Mother! Now, that's more like it."

But her eyes close again.

Enough. It's too tiring.

She blanks out the voices. She concentrates fiercely. His face. She wants to see His face again. But what she sees is Ashton, Ashton in summer as the sun begins to wane.

Twilight is softening the shabbiness of the old house. The big white columns gleam wide and elegant; porches stretching upstairs and down, welcoming family and friends, even strangers. Ah, Ashton. She feels calm, contented. She wants to be at Ashton. She sees Mama standing in the doorway. Papa steps up behind her. *Ashton!*

The Sisters

❦

Ashton Plantation, 1910

"LUCY?" HER FATHER'S VOICE COULD carry without being raised. Oh, it was so hard to put down her book. But no one disobeyed that voice. She marked her place with a feather and quickly rose.

"Coming, Papa."

"You girls know these are indoor hours. Come out of the sun. Where's Sally?"

"I don't know, sir."

Sally was swimming with the Connant boys in Acorn Pond. Lucy was sworn to secrecy and no inquisitor could have wrenched the information from her. Not only was Sally out in the summer sun at mid-afternoon, she was swimming unattended by an adult—with boys. If Papa should find out...

Lucy felt her heart thumping hard when she left the shade of the enormous old oak and slowly made her way toward the house. Not even Mama could save Sally if she were caught this time.

Lucy had begged her sister. "Please don't go, Sally. It's not worth it—oh, please. Papa'll surely find out. You know he always—."

"Ted has dared me and I'm going. With all the excitement about the Remingtons coming, I won't be missed for an hour. You just stay in your tree house and warn me with a coughing fit if anyone's around when I come home."

It was cool and dark inside the old plantation house, the blinds drawn against the harsh sun. White slipcovers were placed over the dulled worn fabrics of the couches and chairs. The ceilings were high, the floors bare and polished to a high gloss. The murmur of female voices drifted from upstairs, a soft clatter of pots and pans from the kitchen mingled with the musical lilt of coastal Negro voices. It could have been 1800.

"Lucy, Lucy, come up here, will you?" The voice was Mary's. "Come on up, stop worrying about Sally, Jenny's crying for you and Lyda wants to get some rest before James and his family arrive."

The six Willoughby girls had a strict and self-imposed hierarchy. Each of the older girls took a younger one under her wing. Lyda, now twenty years old and the cause of the present excitement in the family, had mothered Mary, who was seventeen. Mary had taken on both Sally, eleven, and Lucy, one year younger. When Daphne, age seven, arrived, Sally had reluctantly acted as nursemaid. Lucy was glad that Jenny's care fell to her. Jenny was a jolly three-year-old and Lucy loved her role as assistant mother.

"Where's Mama?" Lucy gathered Jenny into her arms.

"She's with Josephine preparing the feast. Get Jenny down for her nap and let's decide what we'll wear tonight," said Mary.

Lucy heard a gentle tapping on the window.

"Thank heavens—it's Sally."

Here Sally came, blonde hair plastered to her cheeks, blue dress clinging to her budding curves, brown eyes gleaming in her sharp little face.

"Safe again." Lucy pushed up the window leading to the wide upstairs veranda and let her errant sister step through.

"I made it."

"You know, Sally," Lucy said as she combed her hair and smoothed her best dress in preparation of the arrival of Lyda's future inlaws, "it won't be the same here once Lyda gets married. She always had so many beaus.

Sally complained, "We might as well live in the dark ages. Ashton had better have a telephone by the time I'm old enough for beaus."

"But Sally, it's so much fun to *see* who comes calling."

"Here comes someone." Daphne ran into the bedroom she shared with Lucy and Sally.

Sally tucked in her blouse. "Let's go."

As always, Mama waited in the entrance hall, Papa paced among his books nearby.

Papa was an attorney with clients, most of whom paid their fees in barter, and students of the law, whose coin was chiefly admiration and gratitude. Mama's heritage of chipped porcelain, heavy old silver, dark paintings of dour-looking ancestors and modest jewelry was dwindling as she struggled heroically to preserve the illusion that Papa and all attached to him were above worldly acquisitions.

However, the Willoughby girls were sought after by the local swains and could be counted upon to impress any visiting boys as well. Their lively personalities pleased their contemporaries, and their heritage and impeccable manners were just what the mothers wanted for their sons.

On that particular night, the first caller had been a stodgy regular for Mary. When they heard him clear his throat and ask hesitantly if Miss Mary was in, Sally said, "Oh, let's go back to our rooms." But within a half-hour the old parlor was full. The younger girls were sneaking candy from boxes the boys brought. Daphne was playing the piano.

"I'm going for Jenny," Sally whispered.

In a flash, she was back; Jenny, placed on top of the grand piano, was told to perform. Swinging her arms about she began a spirited rendition of the most daring song her sisters had taught her.

"Ain't it a shame, a measly shame, to keep a fella out in the rain."

She continued to much applause and laughter as everyone joined in the singing. Then the dancing began, with the extra boys whirling Sally and Lucy around—Jenny dancing too from her perch on the piano.

"Girls!" Papa's voice stopped them in mid-whirl. "Take Jenny to bed, Lucy. Sally, Daphne, goodnight."

They literally flew from the room. The boys hung back, eyes downcast. Lyda and Mary flushed but stood their ground.

"Now, Colonel," Mama said in a voice soft but firm, "it was just a little joke. I have some lemonade to add to the lovely sweets the boys have brought us. Come on, we'll sit on the porch. Maybe Mary will play an old-fashioned tune especially for us."

Mama never failed to calm Papa down, but she was the only one who could do so. Important people, governors, senators, didn't faze Papa but *Mama!* Lucy loved to hear him tell about the first time he saw Mama when, at the invitation of the headmistress of Darlington Finishing School for Young Ladies, he had ridden over to give the young ladies an hour of instruction on Colonial South Carolina, his favorite era.

"Well, girls," Papa always told the tale in just the same way. "When I saw your mother sitting in the front row with those big blue eyes and that sweet face all surrounded by yellow hair, I was lost right then and there. Yes indeed, my fate was settled. You know very well I'm not easily deterred when I make up my mind. Your mother didn't have a chance."

Mama always interrupted at that point and said, "I didn't want a chance as you certainly realize, Colonel Willoughby. I was simply overwhelmed that such a distinguished older gentleman would take an interest in me."

Mama had led a sheltered life. She was an only child. Her doting father was a physician and therefore not rendered as impoverished by the war as Papa's cotton-growing family had been. Mama had not even been born when General Sherman's troops were burning Columbia, but she had heard the story so often she felt as if she remembered. Her parents, and the small group of loyal black men and women who had stayed right in Darlington with the Abbotts through the whole terrible war, went out into the garden to bury silver and jewelry, then together, they went out and dug it up when Lee surrendered and it was all over.

Now Papa—he had actually fought in the great war, but he didn't talk much about it.

"We must put the war behind us," the Colonel

would say. "It's over. We must rebuild, must do our bit to help *really* unite the States." Papa never hesitated to voice unpopular opinions and start vigorous arguments.

But he didn't mind talking about his mother, Lyda Gerome Willoughby. He wanted his daughters to know all about her because she died before young Lyda was born.

"Next to your mother she was the most remarkable woman in the world," he said. "My father died when I was an infant leaving her alone to manage five boys. I'm ashamed to admit it," Papa even *looked* downcast when he told this part, "but I gave my sainted mother more trouble than all four other boys put together. I was always getting punished for misbehaving in school, and other...transgressions, but mother never lost confidence in me. That made all the difference."

"Then the war—Of course nothing would do for me but to join the fighting once I turned sixteen. The four older brothers were cavalry men. You girls know that the oldest one, George, was killed at Mannassas; your Uncle Ed lost his leg at Brandywine. Poor mother. My leaving almost finished her, but when she saw I was determined, she got a makeshift uniform ready and she called for Charlie, her most trusted servant. Sent that poor man off with me, saying, 'take care of my Johnny for me, Charlie. I count upon you, you know that I do.'

"She cleared out the larder, giving us what provisions she could and off we went—Charlie and myself, on foot. I'd wanted to join the cavalry like my brothers but we didn't have a horse left, just two old plow mules. Still, Charlie and I headed for the fighting and we found it." Here he would stop.

But he never tired of telling the tale of his romance with Mama.

"I should think your mother's parents were less than enchanted when I declared my intentions to Dr. Abbott. Mrs. Abbott was a very elegant Charlestonian. You girls missed two great ladies by not knowing your grandmothers. Nonetheless, I presented myself, a poor country lawyer, and asked for the hand of their treasured darling."

"John, you know they were charmed by you, just like everyone else," Mama would say. "Besides, our families had been friends for generations. That counts for a lot, girls, and don't you forget it!

"More likely, John, it was your mother and brothers who were concerned—a petted and indulged eighteen-year-old for their Johnny's helpmate in life."

"No, Bet, my mother was too wise for that. She recognized character and intelligence when she encountered it."

That's the way the story always unfolded.

"Mama and Papa have a mutual admiration society," Lyda explained to the younger sisters.

* * *

And now Lyda had her own romance. Mama and Papa were certainly an example of enduring love but Lyda was young and pretty and James, whom Lyda had chosen from her many admirers, was handsome and dashing. The sisters were entranced.

When the big grandfather clock in the upstairs hall struck eight o'clock, the Willoughbys were ready.

Lyda stood by her mother. Slightly behind them, the other sisters lined up according to seniority, Mary, Sally, Lucy, Daphne and then Jenny, held in the arms of Dukie, the nursemaid.

In their pastel dresses the girls looked like so many summer lilies, half with blonde hair, half dark, some with blue eyes, some brown, but all with features in some combination of their fiery dark father and his cool blonde wife. The Willoughbys were an impressive group. Their country charm and confidence eclipsed their worn surroundings. They were South Carolina aristocrats, anyone's equal, descended on all sides from early settlers—an Abbott had signed the Declaration of Independence, a Willoughby had been a Colonial Governor.

And so, on this summer night in 1910, the Willoughbys assembled to graciously welcome the new members into their family even though they were North Carolinians and could not, as such, reasonably be expected to be quite up to snuff.

Mrs. Remington of Wilmington stepped out of her carriage to meet the family of her son's intended. Colonel Willoughby marched up and offered her his arm. Pretty Lyda came forward, her mother by her side, and James Remington came behind his mother. The engagement evening began. The first of the Willoughby girls prepared to leave the time-worn mansion that would always be their home.

Lucy

LUCY HAD NO MEMORY OF a time when she didn't know Tom Thornton. He and his brothers lived in nearby Ellerton. Since his parents were friends of Mama and Papa, it was natural that the boys be brought along when the Thorntons came to spend a day or evening at Ashton. The boys loved roaming about in the woods with the more active sisters trailing behind them.

Lucy, not one of the tomboys, would slip away to read. Looking back, she sometimes thought books had been her real life. Heaven knows how many hours she had spent absorbed in them. Papa had a vast library he had gathered from his family and Mama's. Everything saved from the war, everything printed on almost any subject that he could afford to purchase, might turn up in Papa's library. Lucy and her sisters, (all except Daphne who was not a great reader like the others) had read every novel on the shelves. Lucy started with *Little Women* but soon graduated to Dickens.

"Try Thackeray," Mama suggested, and she had loved *Vanity Fair*.

"You should read *Pride and Prejudice*," Mama said. After that she went straight through Jane Austen.

Then Papa took a hand. "Lucy, you should be ready for Sterne. Start with *Tristram Shandy*. What a feast! At Ashton extensive reading was not only allowed but encouraged. Exercise in the fresh air, duties done, then the girls could read. The Willoughby girls were to reach adulthood as knowledgeable in literature and history as anyone they later encountered.

The history came easily, in monologues by Papa. He could bring it all alive. Hearing Papa tell about the Roman Empire or the American Revolution, or indeed almost anything, was like going to a play. Papa was as good an actor as he was a teacher.

Lucy loved to watch him while he talked. Short, compact, with dark flashing eyes, thick grey hair and a bushy salt and pepper mustache, he would occasionally rise from the table to gesture and demonstrate during his dissertations. He exuded energy. Lucy thought Papa was the most positive person she knew. He never wavered. Around him she felt safe and sure. Sally was like him, although she never liked it when Lucy told her so. Her eyes flashed just like Papa's and she moved so quickly and so surely.

"Oh hush, Lucy," Sally would say. "Just because

you're graceful and quiet like Mama and *tall*, you don't have to imply that I'm like Papa!"

But Tom. Tom who had been her friend as long as she could remember, never failed to seek her company when the Thorntons came to visit. He would find her, sit down and try to start a conversation. Poor boys—when it came to conversation, it was almost always up to the girls. Mama had taught her daughters that it was a female duty to keep up the chatter and create the illusion that the males were conversing. So Lucy looked up at Tom with her big blue eyes and managed to make him think he was charming.

He fell hard in love at ten years old and never even looked closely at another girl. But there were always other boys looking at Lucy.

* * *

It wasn't long before Sally was chomping at the bit to join the parlor evenings and have real beaus. "Please, Mama, the boys come to see us anyway. We might as well have the fun of dressing up."

"Oh, Mama, just let us try," Lucy said. "Mary will be right there."

"Well, why not?" Papa said. "Maybe you'll calm down, Miss Sally, and start behaving like a lady."

So at fourteen and fifteen years old, respectively, Lucy and Sally put up their hair, cinched in their waists, and were "at home" on Saturday evenings and Sunday afternoons.

There were still no telephones, so the Willoughby girls lounged about in their rooms, pretending indifference. But to Mama's considerable satisfaction, there was never a girl without at least one caller.

In fact, Lucy saw Mama smile contentedly at a remark old Mrs. Smith made to the hard-of-hearing Mrs. Bellinger when the three ladies were chaperoning a small dance,

"Just look at those Willoughbys taking all the boys."

Mrs. Bellinger's and Mrs. Smith's daughters were still seated and glancing furtively about for rescue. "Well," Mrs. Bellinger attempted a whisper, "there's never been an Abbott female without that quality that nowadays they call "It." I myself would be very concerned if I were Elizabeth Abbott with all those males swarming around my daughters."

The height of social activity at Ashton came with Sally's and Lucy's entrance on to the scene. Boys came from Columbia, Charleston, Greenville.

Tom stood his ground, always there. Lucy took his devotion for granted. She was having too much fun to give it much thought.

* * *

One fall weekend several years later, when Sally and Lucy had completed their sketchy educations at country schools and little Ellerton College for Women, the sisters set forth on the train for a visit with Charleston cousins.

"I love Charleston," Sally said. "Just think what fun those girls have, sneaking puffs off cigarettes and sips from the men's flasks. Really, Lucy, we're so old-fashioned at Ashton."

Lucy knew that Sally was ripe for the meeting when she was introduced to Crawford Carsworth IV, handsome, dashing, and "fast." He pursued her to Ashton; she returned to Charleston.

When he rushed off to join the Army as soon as World War I began, Sally accepted his ring and caused a tumult at Ashton.

Mama, trying to forestall a confrontation with Papa, came into Sally's and Lucy's room for what she announced would be a serious conversation.

"I want Lucy to stay," Sally said. "I know it's about Crawford and I know you don't like him."

"It isn't that, Sally," Mama said quietly. "Of course I like Crawford—who could not? He's charming. I liked his father, who was charming too. But you must realize he drinks far, far more than is—"

"Mother, everyone—"

"Now just let me finish, dear. I know lots of young men drink, but this is different."

"How?" Sally said. "Everyone drinks now except us."

"You need to listen to me on this, Sally. Inheritance is important."

"Inheritance, blood lines, old families—I'm sick of it all. It's not slave and master time on the old plantation, it's a new day."

"Sally, please hear me out." Mama's voice was firm now. She too was accustomed to being obeyed.

"Crawford's blood lines go back to Colonial days, just like ours, that's not the point. We're talking about traits, and traits are inherited."

"But Mama, there are exceptions—"

"Crawford's no exception. Alcohol has ruined the last three generations of Carsworths and it will ruin Crawford's life, too. He shows the signs already. Please reconsider, Sally. Papa and I want only your happiness."

Why couldn't her parents see that the more opposition Sally met, the more determined she became? Lucy could see it. Sally intended to marry Captain Crawford Hamilton Carsworth IV in October, when he had his next leave from the army. She had a large diamond ring, miraculously saved from the pawnbrokers and now adorning her third finger, left hand. And once Papa started in on her, there'd be no chance at all of her turning back. Which may have had something to do with what happened between Lucy and Tom, who made a date to take her for a ride in his father's best buggy.

"Please marry me, Lucy. No one else can ever love you as much as I do."

"Tom, I'm only eighteen, that's too young. I'm not ready to be married."

"Then just take my ring and promise to wait for me until after the war. Please. You know I'll devote the rest of my life to making you happy."

He too had joined the army and was stationed at nearby Camp Jackson, in Columbia.

Lucy sighed. She certainly liked Tom best among her beaus. But, occasionally, she wondered why. Was it just because he was a big, nice-looking man who seemed to love her so very much, and because Mama and Papa so thoroughly approved of him?

Tom pressed and pressed. And at last Lucy gave in and accepted the small sapphire ring that had been his grandmother's.

He kissed her then, trying to get her into his arms and his lips squarely on hers. He'd tried kisses many times before, mostly achieving her cheek or forehead, but as her fiancé, he was clearly entitled to a real kiss.

From the first she felt an odd reluctance about it all. She hesitated to discuss her reservations even with Sally. Sally was so passionate about everything, so headstrong and self-confident. Perhaps by nature she herself was placid and unemotional. Perhaps she would never feel things as Sally did.

She put off setting a date, telling Tom they would

settle on one after Sally and Crawford's wedding.

"There's no rush," Tom said. "We'll wait until the war's over."

Ashton, July 4, 1918

The great war to end all wars was underway but the predominately female Willoughby household was affected only peripherally, through husbands and beaus. Papa's mealtime harangues now centered on military strategy rather than on historical events.

Papa was still quite carried away with the woman's suffrage issue. "Ridiculous," said Papa, "half the population unable to vote. Can't be tolerated, must be changed."

Papa wrote long letters to newspapers deploring the unfairness of the situation. He accepted invitations to speak on the subject and traveled the South at his own expense propounding his views, which were quite unpopular in this part of the country.

"Mark my words, girls, when this war ends women will get the vote."

"Oh, Papa." His daughters would exchange exasperated glances, but only when they were quite sure he wouldn't see them.

But at this time the girls were more concerned with the heightened excitement in their usually predictable lives as men from nearby Camp Jackson enlivened the larger parties. Many of the young men now appeared in uniform rather than dinner jackets.

On the morning of July 4th Lucy and Sally were alone in their cavernous old bedroom getting dressed for a barbecue at the neighboring plantation of Hillstone.

"I'm telling you, Lucy, I'm getting this hair cut and curled the minute Crawford and I get home from our honeymoon. Who could look stylish with this old-fashioned hair Papa makes us keep? Honestly, why we let that man dictate to us, I'll never know. That's what I love about Crawford. He likes a good time and lets me do things my way."

Lucy pushed back any thoughts of her own impending marriage and stepped up to take her place at the mirror. A flush of pleasure rose to her cheeks— pleased at her appearance.

"Oh, Lucy," Sally said. "I wish I had your figure. You're tall and slim and elegant. You can even get by with that awful long hair because yours is so thick and dark. Why do you suppose Mary and Lyda don't cut theirs? I think they're still afraid of Papa. There's Lyda all the way up in North Carolina with three children and still afraid of that tyrant. I do believe that's it."

"Sally, you adore him just like all the rest of us. You know perfectly well nothing feels as uncomfortable as disappointing Papa, and no one can make you feel more wonderful than Papa when you've pleased him."

"Yes, well," Sally said, "let's hurry. Crawford and Tom are waiting downstairs. I heard Crawford's Ford drive up. I hear it's going to be the biggest barbecue we've ever had, with lots of people from the camp and all over. It's a good thing Hillstone is so huge."

Lucy, Sally and their young men piled into Crawford's model-T for the short drive to Hillstone. When they arrived, the wide lawn that swept up toward the rambling old wooden mansion was filled with pastel-dressed women and seersucker-coated men, and a liberal sprinkling of olive uniforms.

Tom took Lucy's arm and they began to maneuver their way across the wide yard toward the shade of a tent that was set up near the broad veranda of the house. They stopped every few steps to greet friends and acquaintances.

Then she saw him—the golden head above the others on the crowded porch. White teeth gleamed in his sunburned face as he smiled down at his companion. He looked up. He looked straight at her. Their eyes locked. Never had she seen eyes so blue. She watched the laughter die from them and a strange intense look take its place. She felt a thrill of excitement so strong she lost her breath for just a second.

She tore her eyes away. What was the matter with her? Her heart was thumping so, she thought surely Tom would notice. But he was casually chatting with the Brewers, his hand still lightly under her elbow.

I won't look up again.

But she did. And met those blue eyes dead on. They must have never left her face. She felt a flush rise from neck to forehead. She saw lieutenant bars gleaming on his shoulders, saw it was Alicia Smith from Columbia by his side. Lucy edged toward the veranda, her body moving toward his as if propelled by an outside force. She dared not look up, she felt so very odd.

"Why, hello Alicia," she heard Tom say. "How nice that you could come over for the day."

He must have been walking forward just as she was. She lifted her head and met his gaze again. She had never seen a look of such intensity. It was impossible to look away. The excitement was almost unbearable.

"Lucy," Alicia said, "have you met Adam? Adam, this is Lucy Willoughby. This is my fiancé, Adam Stover."

Fiancé! She tried to speak but no words would come and she must say something, what would they think? What was the matter with her?

"Miss Willoughby," he said, "my pleasure." Even his voice was special, deep, the accent not southern but elegant, perhaps New England.

"And this is Lucy's fiancé, Lieutenant Tom Thornton."

Lucy watched his face. Oh, yes—she saw it. The light left his face. How strange it all was.

The men shook hands and then he looked at her again, straight into her eyes. The moment lengthened.

"Well," Alicia said with an artificial little laugh, "we'd best go meet some of the other neighbors, Adam. That's what we came for, after all."

"Nice looking fella," Tom said. "I've seen him at the camp. I think he's from near Boston, left Harvard to attend Officers' School, very pleasant for a Yankee. Crawford knows him."

Lucy moved as in a dream but the euphoria was now gone. Still, her heart beat in double time. She felt flushed with heat. Everything she saw seemed clearer and brighter than normal.

"Miss Willoughby, won't you have this glass of lemonade?" He was right beside her, smiling down. "Although you look as cool and fresh as the proverbial daisy, you must surely be thirsty?"

"Why, thank you, Lieutenant Stover. I am warm, and if a South Carolinian feels the heat, how you must be suffering." She smiled up at him and heard his breath catch.

"You are the most beautiful girl I've ever seen in all my life," he said in a low intense voice, his eyes now on her lips.

"Oh, Lieutenant Stover, a Yankee shouldn't exercise such bold charm on a poor country girl. We don't know how to cope with sophistication." She was *flirting* and they were both engaged. She still felt the heat in her cheeks.

"Miss Willoughby." He took her elbow. It felt like an electric shock. She looked dead at him and he looked back. There was no mistaking it, he felt what she did. His face was strained as if he were in pain.

"Oh, there you are, Adam." It was Alicia. "I think we should get a bite to eat now. Sam and Louise are saving us a seat on the north porch, the coolest spot."

"Out of deference to his Yankee blood, no doubt," Lucy said.

She had never liked Alicia but now she felt the purest loathing—that spoiled only child, growing up in Columbia with lots of money! No wonder Sally had been so determined to win whenever she and Alicia competed for beaus and attention.

"Would you like to see my ring?" Alicia thrust her hand toward Lucy. It was a large emerald-cut diamond.

"Beautiful," Lucy murmured. She couldn't look at him. She never wanted to see him again. She wanted to die right there on the spot. But he didn't move.

"Miss Willoughby," he said with great intensity, "tell me, is your home nearby?" Her resolve melted. They looked at each other, eyes drawn as if by magnets.

"Yes, about a mile east of here. It's called Ashton."

"A pretty name," he said. "I like the way the old

homes around here all have names and, really, personalities. I hope I'll see Ashton some day."

"We're being rude to our hostess, Adam, come on." Alicia was actually pulling him this time.

Lucy picked at the fried chicken and the fresh tomatoes on her plate as she sat between Tom and Crawford. She could scarcely swallow. Indeed, she felt sick. How could he be engaged to that shallow, vain woman? And poor Tom. She was no more aware of him than her surroundings.

"What a wonderfully handsome man Alicia has gotten hold of," Sally said. "How long has he been at the camp?"

"About six months," Crawford said. "He met Alicia at a dance the Flemings gave as a morale booster for the officers from other states. And she lost no time in setting her cap. We hear his family owns woolen mills and are rich. But he's a gentleman—fits in well."

What terrible, rotten luck—if *she* could have been at that dance!

"Miss Willoughby." He was beside her chair. "It seems we must leave now if we're to be back in Columbia in time for supper. It's been such a pleasure to meet you and Lieutenant Thornton."

"Lieutenant," he turned to Tom. "I'll look forward to seeing you at the post."

"Of course." Tom rose to shake hands. "Let me introduce you to Miss Sally Willoughby, I believe you know her fiancé, Crawford Carsworth?" Chairs scraped back and more handshaking took place.

"I see a resemblance," he said with a smile. "You must be sisters."

"Yes, we are," Sally said in her lively way. "But most people think we look the least alike. Lucy looks like Lyda. They could be twins."

"I hope I'll have the pleasure of meeting the beautiful Lyda." His eyes were back on Lucy, who met his gaze and felt her cheeks flame. Even Tom could not have failed to see the intensity of that exchange. Then Alicia came and took his arm and they were gone.

* * *

"Lucy," Sally whispered, when they were back in their room, "what in the world is going on with you and that handsome Yankee lieutenant? I never saw such looks as you gave each other. Alicia will have you skinned alive. Were you flirting with him? That's not like you."

"Oh, Sally, let's just don't talk about it," Lucy said, then burst into tears and sobbed herself to sleep in Sally's arms.

She tried not to think about him. It was all too absurd. She must have had a touch of heatstroke. But his face stayed with her. The few words they had exchanged echoed in her ears. Perhaps she'd imagined his interest in her, the emotion in his voice.

Even if she hadn't imagined it, how could she do this to Tom?

What was wrong with her?

On Saturday morning, she was stripping the bed linens, preparing to help Dukie with the upstairs chores, when the bedroom door flew open and Sally burst in.

"Good heavens, Lucy, your Yankee lieutenant is here."

"Where? Oh, Sally—"

"He's right there in the sitting room talking to Papa. He said he's interested in antebellum architecture in the South and presumed to drop by, being in the area, to see if he might get a look at Ashton. Mama's freshening up to go down. Come on, come on. Of course, he came to see you. You should have seen the look he gave me. I was almost hypnotized into coming for you."

Lucy flew to the long mirror and began to smooth her hair. "Oh, Sally, hurry, hurry. Hand me that blue cotton dress. I think it's becoming, don't you?"

Her heart was thumping and her face flushed up. She pushed down her guilty feelings. *I don't care, I don't care, what harm can it do for me to see him once again?*

When she reached the stairs, she paused at the top, took a deep breath and began to walk slowly.

"Come on, Jenny," she said. "Take my hand and we'll see who's come to visit."

It would seem more casual if several sisters dropped in together. But still her heart was beating double time, she was going to see him again!

He sprang to his feet when she came in the room, his face alight.

"Why, Miss Willoughby, how delightful to see you again. This lovely young lady must be another sister. Perhaps you two could show me the grounds and verandas?"

Papa took his arm. "Come, I'll show you around myself. Delighted to have a Bostonian take an interest in our little neck of the woods. Girls, fix a pot of coffee for the Lieutenant and myself and we'll have it later in the upstairs parlor."

"Yes, Papa." Lucy and Sally exchanged despairing glances.

"I'll help Josie with the coffee," Sally said. "Go get Mama and brush up the parlor. He'll come back in, you'll see."

And indeed he did. He stepped right into the shabby old upstairs parlor, a little glaze of perspiration on his handsome brow, the stiff uniform with just a slightly crushed look. His expression was intense. His eyes flew straight to Lucy.

Papa said, "This is my wife, Lieutenant Stover."

He bowed over Mama's hand. "What a pleasure to meet you, Mrs. Willoughby, and to be in your beautiful home—such kindness to a stranger. I can see that the Southern reputation for hospitality is well deserved."

"Well, now," Papa said. "We aren't strangers. What do you think, Bet, dear?" He turned to Mama. "Lieutenant Stover is a cousin of my dear friend, Professor Adams, at Harvard and will take him my personal regards when he goes back North."

"How nice," Mama said. "And will you leave soon, Lieutenant? Aren't you the Lieutenant Stover who is engaged to Alicia Smith, Sally's friend from Columbia?"

His face changed. "Yes, Mrs. Willoughby," he said softly, "I am."

There was a moment's silence as Mama looked at him, calmly but quite steadily. He straightened his shoulders and met her gaze but his face now appeared quite stricken. Even Papa seemed to notice.

"Well, now, how about a cup of coffee or perhaps a glass of lemonade? I see we have both," he said.

"Thank you very much."

Oh, he's waiting to be asked to sit down. Mama, do ask him to sit down.

"Come sit by me, Lieutenant Stover," Mama said, "and tell me about your home and family in Massachusetts."

Ah, he moved so quickly yet so gracefully.

"Well, we live in a small village near Boston. Actually, the house is much like this. We don't have the columns or wide porches, of course, and the ceilings are not so high but the furnishings and general appearance remind me very much of home. In fact, I feel at home here, Mrs. Willoughby, and I thank you so much for permitting this intrusion. You see, there are two sisters and myself in our family, so I miss the company of ladies as well as the comforts of home."

Then he turned slightly so that he could see Lucy and his face changed again. He looked happy. In fact, his face glowed. Their eyes stayed on each other. Their remarks must have been normal. Later Sally said they were. But Lucy did not remember what was said. Occasionally, he would wrench his gaze away and look at her father. For once, Lucy was glad Papa was so garrulous. It relieved the others of the effort small talk would have required.

He stood up. "Do forgive me. I've stayed much too long. How can I thank you for such kindness?"

"Come, young man," Papa said, "I'll walk you to your car."

"Oh Lucy," Sally said quickly, "if you don't mind going down, would you bring me that long-handled feather duster? I need it if we are going to finish our chores today."

Lucy jumped up to accompany the men.

Papa led the way, with Lucy and the Lieutenant behind. Papa made the turn in the stairs and disappeared for a second. The Lieutenant turned toward her. He grasped her hand and brought it to his lips.

She thought she might faint. She felt so strange,

so hot and melting, breathless and strangling. Of course Tom and, to tell the truth, some other boys, too, had kissed her on the lips. But never had she felt like this. Oh, dear Lord, what was she to do?

They rounded the curve and he dropped her hand, but she heard his labored breathing and was afraid to glance at him.

They reached the back porch. As Papa strode through the door, she stopped and held the screen open for the Lieutenant.

"Goodbye," she said and met his eyes.

"Lucy," he whispered, then more loudly, "goodbye and thank you again."

He was gone with a roar of his fancy motor car, the grandest car she had ever seen.

* * *

Lucy moved slowly through the next few days. Voices were faint; familiar sights seen only dimly. Her world shifted on its axis. Tom, even Mama and Papa—all were seen as through a haze, only *he* was clear and real.

Sally said, "I think you've fallen in love with this Yankee man. Nothing can possibly come of it. Please, Lucy, don't set your heart on this. He's different and wonderfully handsome, that's what's mesmerized you. Alicia will never let him go, and poor Tom."

Lucy turned blind eyes on her sister and moved as though sleepwalking.

A few days later, Daphne came bursting into their room. "Lucy, Lucy. You've got a letter from the camp and I don't think it's from Tom. And a note has come for Mama and Papa with a huge bunch of florist flowers all the way from Columbia."

Sally snatched the letter. "Are you a private detective or some such, Miss Nosey? Let Lucy investigate her own letter. Lucy, come on, sit down."

My Dear Miss Willoughby,
My friends, Captain and Mrs. Clayton, will be
driving to Ellerton next Saturday and want to
look at some of the plantations. Could we stop by
Ashton at about four o'clock and perhaps have the
pleasure of yours and Miss Sally's company when
we go to see Hillstone?

Sincerely,
Adam Stover

Postscript
I have written your parents under separate cover
to thank them again for their exceptional hospital-
ity to a stranger.

"Oh, Sally, look. I *will* see him again." And that thought filled her whole being.

On Saturday, Lucy spent the rest hour on her toilette. Dresses were tried and passed over. Finally, with Sally assisting, she decided on a lavender dotted Swiss with a wide ribbon cummerbund that displayed her slender waist. The color made her eyes look especially blue.

"Darling Sally," Lucy said. "Thank you, thank you for giving up your afternoon with Crawford to go with us. You know Papa would never have let me go if you weren't going too, even if Captain and Mrs. Clayton are along."

"You do things for me all the time. Of course, I'd go. Besides, he's fascinating and so smitten, it's pitiful. But, Lucy, I'm warning you. You've got to get hold of yourself and stop this thing, *two* engagements."

"I know, Sally, I know."

"And Lucy, that spoiled, selfish Alicia will hang on for all she's worth. He's so handsome and cultivated and he must be rich as well, that automobile and his family owning mills. It's hopeless, this will have to be the last time you see him."

"I know, I know. Imagine you being the cautious one. I just have to see him one more time. I understand and agree with you, truly I do, Sally. Let's wait on the porch so Papa won't get hold of them."

* * *

As the car rounded the curve in the red clay road, Lucy's heart rose up. It was almost in her throat and beating alarmingly. He sprang out the minute the motor stopped.

"Miss Lucy, Miss Sally, how kind of you to go with us. Let me introduce my friends from Boston."

Oh my, what an elegant couple. Lucy's smile faltered for just a moment. Mrs. Clayton had on a dress of such simple elegance, navy blue with white trim, a cloche hat, bobbed hair. New York City was stamped all over her. Lucy glanced at Sally, who was all smiles. Sally loved style and elegance. Her sacrifice of the afternoon would be well worthwhile.

Captain Clayton stood by the back door, quite elegant looking himself but older and not so tall or handsome as the lieutenant.

"Miss Sally, perhaps you would join my wife and myself on the back seat," Captain Clayton offered.

Lucy sank down on the front seat beside the lieutenant. She was so happy, so happy. Never had she felt so alive. Only this moment mattered.

"I think it would be nice," Sally said, "if we dispensed with formality and pretend we're old friends. That's the only way to manage in this awful war with people being shuffled around so. Please call me Sally and my sister's Lucy."

"Oh, yes," he said. "Thank you so much, Miss— I mean Sally. I'd be so pleased if you both call me Adam. This is Hannah and the captain's Alexander. But if we're really friends, call him Alec."

Sally and Hannah began a lively exchange of small talk. Turning so that she might add a word or two enabled Lucy to see Adam's profile as he drove—chiseled features, soft looking yellow hair. She felt quite faint and looked away, heart thumping. When she faced forward again, he looked at her. He tightened his hands on the wheel and wrenched his eyes away just as a curve approached.

As they rounded the curve leading to Hillstone, Sally said, "Here we are. We sent that boy of Dukie's with a note telling the Firestones that we would come for a walk around. Hope he made it. Anyway, only Miss Nell and Miss Gwen are here and they'll be asleep at this hour. Amos will be about and can show us the old wine house and water cistern. Of course, Yankees, even such nice ones as yourselves, will want to see the remains of the slave quarters and observe for yourselves the depravity of our antebellum days."

Lucy caught the touch of bitterness that showed in the last sentence. Even blithe, Sally was displaying a little of the resentment of the old defeat and humiliating occupation that was passed from generation to generation in the South. Sally fell in step with the Claytons and led them to the rear of the large rambling house, where indeed some remaining slave quarters still stood.

Adam stood beside Lucy, quite close, his arm brushing hers. His hand, hard and brown, closed about her elbow.

"Lucy," he began. "Do forgive me. You must think I'm insane pursuing you this way. I had to see you again. I can't stop myself from this bizarre behavior, Lucy, Lucy."

Adam's eyes stayed on her face. She was afraid to look at him. They stood with the others but they were unaware of anything but each other. Sally kept up a steady stream of chatter and it was all over, too, too soon.

Back at Ashton, Sally asked them to come inside for iced tea. The Claytons turned to Adam, who was already accepting. Of course, Mama and Papa were waiting in the living room. Lucy could have wept with frustration. She wanted so much to be alone with him. Oh, if she could have just one hour alone with him, then maybe she would be all right.

Finally the Claytons rose at last and the afternoon was over.

* * *

The next note arrived on Monday.

Dear Lucy,
I must see you alone, if only for a few minutes.
I'll be able to get away this coming Sunday after-
noon. Could you possibly meet me at three o'clock
at the turn of your driveway, just for a few min-
utes? I'll be waiting.
—A.S.

Sally said, "Don't do it, Lucy. You're getting involved. There'll be nothing but heartbreak in this for you."

"I can't explain it," Lucy said, "but I tell you I would give ten years of my life to be alone with him for ten minutes. I know that sounds theatrical and absurd but I mean it. I've got to see him. Help me. You and I could stroll off together while the others are resting. If anyone should happen to notice we could say we needed a breath of fresh air."

"All right, I'll do it, but remember Tom and Crawford are coming over at five o'clock. And imagine what anyone would think of us walking out for fresh air in July heat in mid-afternoon. We have to hope Mama and Papa and tattletale Daphne fall fast asleep after dinner."

She was awake at dawn Sunday morning. The day dragged. Church was endless, although a boring sermon by old Mr. Phipps presented her with a chance to daydream.

His face, if only she could touch it once. What was she thinking of? She must be depraved.

At dinner, she pushed the food around on her plate, pretending to eat. Was Mama noticing? She had a way of knowing what was going on with each and every girl. Lucy made an effort to smile and join in the conversation.

At last, it was time. As she and Sally rounded the curve of the driveway, they saw his automobile, set well back off the dirt road.

"Goodness, he's parked in the *woods*," Sally said.

"All right now, Lucy, I'm going back. You've covered up for me enough times. I owe you this. But don't stay long, and for heaven's sake be quiet as a mouse when you come in."

He was standing by the car looking very warm and very anxious. His face lit up when he saw her. He rushed forward.

"You came, I was so afraid you wouldn't, I was terrified you'd decide I'm crazy, I know I'm acting that way."

He stood very close to her. She felt his breath on her face when she looked up.

"Lucy."

"There's a nice little stream down here through these trees," she said. "It cools things off a bit. We could talk for a minute there. Truly, I can't stay but a few minutes. If I'm missed, we'll both be judged insane. Papa has the most terrible temper. Really, Adam, I'm quite afraid of him. I don't know why, because he's certainly never raised a hand against any of us, he disapproves of corporal punishment, even for unruly boys, but then no punishment is necessary—he speaks and we obey."

Good heavens, she was so nervous, she was babbling like an idiot. What must he think?

"Look at this," he said. "The tree trunk is almost a bench. Could we sit down for just a moment? Would you excuse me if I take off my jacket? It'll make a cushion."

His shoulders were broad, the starched shirt stretched tight across them. Her heart began that strange pounding again. She longed to touch him. She had never dreamed of such feelings.

"I apologize for putting you in this position," he said. "I can't forgive myself but I can't stop. Lucy, I'm not as young as you and haven't been sheltered as girls are. I've considered myself in love several times in my years at Harvard and, of course, just recently. But, I tell you most truly, I've never felt this way before."

"No, Adam, no—you shouldn't say any more."

But he just stepped closer. "I'm bewitched. I've thought of nothing but you since the day I saw you. I can't eat or sleep or work. I'm obsessed—you must help me, I'm ill with longing to be with you."

He was looking straight down at her and oh, he was so close. She felt his warm breath again. She looked quickly away. He mustn't read her scandalous thoughts.

She turned and sat down on his jacket, then he sat close beside her.

"Adam, I came to tell you that, of course, we mustn't be alone together again. We're both engaged."

"I know, I know. I never thought I could be capable of behaving in such a dishonorable fashion. But my feelings are too strong to be ignored. I must know, Lucy, do you feel just a little of what I do?"

"Oh, Adam, more than a little."

"Darling." His face lit up. He took her hand and pressed his lips into her palm.

Oh, her hand on his face, just as she had dreamed. His jaw was hard and slightly rough.

"Lucy, I'm in love with you. I promised myself I wouldn't say it and frighten you away. But I can't stop myself." He was breathing quickly—his grip on her hand tightened. He jumped up and stepped away. "I know I'm behaving like the worst sort of cad. I'm betraying my promise to Alicia, being a traitor to Tom, a fellow officer, and worst of all, putting you in a terrible position.

"But Lucy, I love you desperately. I know it's sudden but it's the truest emotion I've ever felt. I'll never get over this. Lucy, could you love me, too, just a little?"

She rose and stood beside him. To flirt and temporize never entered her mind. The years of training and practice fell away. "Adam, I've never felt so strangely or so strongly. It surely must be that I love you, too."

He turned and drew her into his arms. Then he bent his head and kissed her—kissed her right on her mouth! She was pressed to his hard chest. She felt his hammering heart beat. She melted against him, breathless, blinded. She clung to him and kissed him back. The kiss went on and on.

"My God!" He dropped his arms and broke away. His voice was unsteady, his breathing audible.

She felt bereft. Oh, now, now she understood, she knew why whispered-about women ruined themselves for some man; she'd have walked right off with him then and there and gone to the camp or a hotel or any place on earth just to stay with him.

"My God," he said again. "Can you ever forgive me?" He was still breathing hard. "I lost my head. I've taken advantage of your youth and innocence. I'd rather die than hurt you. Oh, Lucy—Lucy."

She was trembling, but she made a big effort to speak naturally. "I must go. You probably think I'm a hopeless flirt or something worse. We can't ever meet again."

She turned and ran down the path. He was beside her in a second and grasped her arm.

"No, I'll not lose you. We aren't married yet, thank God. This can be worked out. Please, Lucy, please. I can come again at the same time next week. Promise you'll come once more and hear me out."

She was running now, with him beside her taking great strides and holding fast to her arm. He turned her to him and locked her eyes with his.

"Promise me, Lucy."

"Yes, I'll come."

* * *

On Wednesday afternoon of the interminable week that followed, Sally drew her out on the porch.

"Lucy, Mama knows something's going on. She asked me about you and the lieutenant. You know she never encourages us to betray each other's confidences, but I couldn't deny it. Anyone with eyes can tell something's going on. I'm sure she and Papa have discussed it. I think they figure your judgment is so sound and you're always so good about trying to do the right thing that they can hold off interfering. Now if it were me, can you imagine the carrying on we'd have?"

"Oh, surely they don't know I've seen him alone?"

"No, no, but they know of the letters."

"Sally, help me. I need to keep this private just a little longer."

So Sally helped her, reporting back to Lucy that Mama and Papa were having restrained conversations when their door was closed.

Sally, not even pretending to be ashamed of her eavesdropping, gathered that Papa was in favor of stepping in to have a talk with the lieutenant but Mama was managing to hold him at bay. Mama wanted to give Lucy a little more time to sort it out for herself.

One morning a note came, as always, heralded by Daphne.

Dear Lucy,
I'm almost afraid to write. I may say too much or say the wrong thing and frighten you after all. I must tell you at least this—I'm the happiest man

at Camp Jackson. Now I know what "walking on air" means. You are the most wonderful thing that's ever happened to me, or ever will.

I'm counting minutes until Sunday. Love always, A.

Lucy had trouble sleeping. Eating was almost impossible. She felt at fever pitch all the time.

On Friday, as the girls were gathering on the shaded front porch after their rest, an automobile approached. Daphne, as usual, dashed off to investigate. But Sally was first to recognize their visitor.

"Good heavens, Lucy, it's Alicia."

Sally leaned over the banister and called out, "Come on up, Alicia, so nice of you to drop by."

She turned back to Lucy. "Get prepared now, you know this visit has a purpose. Thank heavens Mama and Papa are out."

"Do sit down, Alicia," Lucy said, "I'll get us some iced tea."

"Oh, no thank you, Lucy, I've only got a moment. I'm going over to Hillstone to call on the dear old ladies. Thought I'd drop by to talk wedding plans with you and Sally. After all, we have so many mutual friends, we should coordinate things. Just when *do* you plan to marry Tom?"

"Oh," Lucy said, her face flushed, "we don't have any definite plans yet. Sometime after Sally and Crawford or when the war's over or, later."

"Crawford and I are planning an October wedding," Sally interjected.

"Well, good. Adam doesn't want to wait. We don't know how long he'll be at the camp. We were thinking of September."

Lucy's vision blurred and the landscape whirled around her. She grasped the banister to steady herself. She was suddenly bathed in icy perspiration.

Alicia's face looked hard, not even pretty now. She stared Lucy down.

"Well, how very, very considerate of you to come all the way over to share your plans with us." Sally was equal to almost any occasion.

Alicia turned her cold blue eyes on Sally.

"It's always best to have things smooth. We all know how distasteful any controversy is to our dear old-fashioned parents."

Tears had come to Lucy's eyes. Oh, she couldn't stand another minute of it. Could she possibly have misunderstood him? She held with both hands to the banister, afraid she might faint.

Sally stepped in between Lucy and Alicia. "How nice of you to be so concerned with others, Alicia, so typical. Maybe we'll run into Lieutenant Stover and be able to tell him about your thoughtfulness," Sally said.

Alicia flushed from neck to forehead.

Oh, she's furious. What have I done? What must I do?

"Well, I'll run on now," Alicia rose and started toward the steps.

"Lucy," she said, and stood until Lucy met her gaze, "I do hope that things will go smoothly for you. We all love dear Tom and would hate to see him upset."

Lucy managed to hold back her tears until the car started away.

"Listen, Lucy." Sally put her arms around her. "This is a mess, no doubt about it. But we're not going to let that horrid, conniving, hypocritical cat bully and maneuver us. You're planning to meet him again. Well, meet him. Then we'll see."

* * *

For the next two days Lucy's emotions and spirits rose and then fell alarmingly. Was she mistaken in Adam? No, no, she was *not*, she would stake her life on Adam. Were they behaving in a very selfish, even immoral way? Yes, maybe so. Certainly it was her duty to renounce him. Poor Tom, poor trusting Mama and Papa. Must she give him up? *Could* she give him up? Would she be punished for her selfishness, or was it maybe even ruthlessness?

But underneath it all she *knew*. She was going to have Adam Stover, nothing was going to stop her, not Alicia or Tom or even Mama and Papa. Adam belonged to her.

* * *

At last it was Sunday.

When Lucy was getting ready to go to Adam, Sally came flying through the doorway.

"Lucy, of all things, Papa has come to me about you and Adam. He likes him, he seems to sort of *approve* of him. I can't believe it. I'd have thought he would have gotten out his old dueling pistols by now.

"He wants to talk to Adam, but I told you, Mama doesn't want him to, she thinks you should come to a decision between Adam and Tom entirely on your own. She thinks it's more dignified to ignore everything until Adam breaks with Alicia and declares himself.

"They trust you so, Lucy, maybe more than any of the rest of us."

Tears stung Lucy's eyes.

If they knew how she felt, what she wanted—

"Lucy," Sally said, "you know it's not some little tempest-in-a-teapot scandal over broken engagements that Mama and Papa are worried about. We've got to hand it to Papa for not caring what other people think. They're worried about you. Dear Lord, if they ever find out you've met him alone and in the woods and you're going again."

But Lucy finished dressing and marched off, without Sally this time.

He was standing by the car just like the week before.

"Lucy, darling." He pulled her into his arms and kissed her quickly right where they stood.

"Oh, Adam, no." She turned and walked very fast toward the stream and tree trunk.

As soon as they stopped, he reached for her again.

"No, Adam. Don't you know what's happened? Alicia came to Ashton."

"Good Lord." He stepped back, his face paling. "What did she want?"

"She obviously knows something's going on but she claimed to want to coordinate our wedding plans, and she said you and she plan to marry in September."

"September! We certainly had no such plan. What could she be thinking of to act this way? I hate this for you, Lucy. Were your parents there?"

"No, thank goodness, they weren't at home, but Sally was with me and certainly held up our end of the exchange."

He jerked off his jacket and tossed it on the tree trunk. "Please let's sit down, Lucy."

He seemed harried, sounded breathless. Lucy sat down on his jacket so that he, too, could sit. He sank down close beside her and said, "Let me explain, I'm not proud of myself in any of this, in fact, I'm downright ashamed. Of course I should have called or written Alicia, but my God, I can hardly seem to remember her, I'm consumed with you.

"I've been on around-the-clock duty at the camp these last two weeks, it's only through Alec's intervention that I could get away for a few hours last Sunday and today.

"Lucy, you must believe this, Alicia and I never had any definite wedding plans, even before I met you. I'm ashamed of this, too, but from the first it was just a wartime thing. I've acted like an irresponsible fool or anything else you can name. Certainly now I know I never loved her."

He pulled out a snowy handkerchief and wiped his forehead. "Do you think you can believe me and trust me?"

"Yes, Adam," she looked straight up at him. "I've made up my mind that I'm going to. I'm not so pleased with myself either. Tom loves me and think how I've betrayed him, I'm deceiving Mama and Papa, I've acted like no decent woman ever would. I hate how I've behaved."

"No, no, Lucy, no! Don't think that way for a moment. It's all my fault, entirely my fault. I'll make it up to you. We have the rest of our lives to make it right."

He kissed her palm and kept his warm face there so long her heart began its wild pounding again. Then he stood up and looked down at her.

"I'm completely in love with you. Nothing else I've ever felt has been so strong as what I feel for you.

"We've got to break off these engagements right away. I'll have to assume the role of the Yankee cad, but if I know Alicia, she'll recover, and quickly. It's you I'm concerned about."

He sat back down, as close as he could get.

"I want you to be very, very sure of your feelings. I know I've pressured and rushed you. But when we're free, if you still feel the same toward me, will you marry me?"

"Yes, Adam, I will."

He kissed her, gently this time, holding her face in his hands.

"I've already written Alicia a note. It will be there when she gets home from Atlanta on Saturday. I'll call on her and her parents that day. Then I'll come straight here and begin to try to make my case with your parents, if you're free by then. How does that sound to you?"

"Yes, yes. I'm seeing Tom tonight and I'll give him back his ring. Mama and Papa will have this week to absorb that. They only want me to be happy and safe."

He stood and began to pace back and forth. "Lucy, we must be prepared for opposition. Your parents will probably be appalled at my nerve. Mine will be disappointed in my ungentlemanly behavior, but when they meet you they'll be charmed and they'll be happy for me." He sat back down and took her hand, again.

"We must be very careful with your parents. I want them to like me and trust me, because you'll never be happy if they're unhappy with me, and I want to spend my life making you happy. I want to give you beautiful things and take you to beautiful places."

"Adam, all I want is to be with you. I know I'm just a young and inexperienced country girl, but what I feel for you is what you said, the truest thing I've ever felt. I love you."

He stood up and pulled her straight into his arms. She was crushed against him and he was kissing her. She closed her arms around his hard back and pressed closer and closer, returning his kisses. She felt him tremble as if in a strong wind.

It was just like last time, she was weak with terrible, wonderful feelings. It was he, once again, who broke away. He pulled her arms from around him, kissed each one in turn, again and again, then her hands.

That was no better. She was still awash with violent feelings. She swayed toward him. He held her off.

"Leaving you now is the hardest thing I've ever done, Lucy. The fact that I'm doing it is the measure of my love for you. Oh, Lucy, my Lucy."

* * *

It was almost dark when she got home. Papa

was in the library but Mama was waiting in the hall.

"Mama, I've got to get ready to see Tom now. I hate to worry you. Oh, Mama, we'll talk later. Everything's fine. Please don't worry."

Mama looked at her glowing face and said not a word.

* * *

Telling Tom was harder than she had thought it would be, but her resolve never wavered.

"I can't tell you how sorry I am to cause you pain, Tom. But I just can't marry you, I really don't love you, it would be wrong. You deserve love and absolute devotion from your wife. You're too fine a person to have less."

"No, no. It's you I want. I'll never love another woman. I've loved you all my life, since we were children. Keep the ring, keep it, put it away for a while, don't make me take it back."

But she did. When he put it in his pocket, tears came to his eyes. Oh, poor, proud Tom. She mustn't let him cry in front of a woman. Her heart was aching and her head was pounding but she didn't relent.

"Forgive me, Tom, when you can. I'll always count you among my dearest and most valued friends."

"I'm not a complete fool, Lucy." Anger had braced him. The tears were gone. "I know who's responsible for this. It's that goddamned Yankee, Stover. It's plain as day from the way he acts. I see him at camp, he looks guilty, he looks guilty as hell. I wish to God we still had duels."

He left at last. His parting words were, "He's not one of us. This won't last. You'll come to your senses, Lucy, and I'll be waiting."

Later, she found her parents together in the library.

"Mama, Papa, please don't ask me to explain and talk about it right now. But I want you to know I've given Tom's ring back."

"Lucy—" Papa began, but for the first time in her life, she interrupted him.

"Please, Papa."

Then another most unusual thing happened, Mama interrupted them both.

"Colonel, I think we should consider Lucy's feelings on this. She's had a hard scene with Tom, I'm sure. Let's all get some rest and discuss it later."

Papa's disapproving look was like a blow but he didn't say another word.

That night in bed, she told the whole story to Sally, who made no further objections. She knew her sister. Underneath Lucy's soft exterior was solid steel. Once she had decided on a course, there would be no dissuading her.

So Sally stayed close and watchful, lending silent support. She and Lucy kept busy. Between them they managed to avoid private conversations with Mama or Papa.

* * *

On Tuesday morning Lucy went to check the mail. She couldn't stop herself. There was no reason to think he would write. He'd explained how busy and pressured he was.

No telephone! How could any community be so backward? This was a new century, a different time. They were so isolated and insular. If only Papa cared as much about convenience as he did about his ideas, he would have *done* something and they might at least have a telephone like everyone else in America.

But when she opened the box there it was—a long thick envelope addressed to her in his handwriting. Her heart began to pound. She sank down on the nearest patch of grass right there with the sun blasting down on her alabaster complexion—strictly forbidden by Mama—and ripped open the envelope and began to read.

Sunday Night

My Darling,
  I felt as if I were tearing off one of my arms or a leg when I left you a few hours ago. But more likely it was my heart. The portion that will make

it whole and healthy will henceforward always be in your hands.

It is the most terrible frustration to have these deadlines on our time together. Things will be better after Saturday but only when this war has ended and you are with me all the time, will I rest easy. I want you to know my family and my plans even if sketchily and by proxy before I present your parents with my marriage proposal.

Lucy, believe me, essentially our families are quite similar. My mother is a real lady, just as your mother is, in the very best sense of that word. You and she will be comfortable together. My father in his way is probably as forceful as yours appears to be. You and he will understand each other. Besides, he has a considerable appreciation of female beauty! My little sisters are like your younger ones. They think everything I do is wonderful. For once, they'll be found correct and they will love and emulate you, which will be a fine thing. We New Englanders are reserved and more formal than Southerners but you can help us there as well.

Since I was a child I've assumed that I would take over the management of our family mills—woolen mills—just as my father took over from his. I like the business, our community, the people who work for us, the whole package but, my dearest, if any of this life plan should make you unhappy, everything can be reconsidered. From this moment on, you come first with me.

However, I think you will enjoy Boston. I think you are absolutely ready to stretch your mind and absorb what a great city has to offer, our symphony, our museums and libraries. I can hardly wait to show you Harvard, so old and venerable. Your father will want to stay there forever—right in the library!

We'll go to New York to the theater and to the shops. We'll walk down Fifth Avenue and I shall buy you something from each and every store. I'll tolerate no opposition on that score. We'll go to Europe. I spent six weeks traveling there with my parents between Groton and Harvard but my heart wasn't in it, just passing time. This will be different. Oh so different.

Now about this war. I was reared to do my duty. My country is at war, of course I want to do my part. But to tell the truth and only to you, darling Lucy, now that I have you (or almost have you!) I've lost my zest for the thing. I had thought my great desire was to go to France and test myself in battle. But no more. I'll go and do my best if required of course. But now my great desire is to survive—to have you.

Forgive me, my Lucy, if this has been tedious. I would so much have preferred to tell you these things in person and over time, rather than all at once. But you need to know something about me. You see, I am already protecting you, even from myself!

*Now, Lucy, will you write to me and tell me
what you think of these plans I've sketched out?
Just tell me anything and everything you have
time to write. Until Saturday then—
Goodnight my love, I do love you so.
—A.*

She kept the letter in her pocket all day.

"Sally," she whispered when they were getting ready for bed. "I got this wonderful letter from Adam today, all about his family and his plans for his life—well, our life together after we've married. I'm going to write him an answer tonight. Will you stop Daphne from complaining so I can have the lamp on late?"

"I'd love to. There's nothing I like better than squelching Daphne. It's just what she needs, the self-centered little flirt."

"Oh, she's not so bad. I think she just feels squeezed out. She's too young for us and too old for Jenny."

"Good heavens, you're just like Mama—always *understanding* other people. You're so good. Well at least you're not goody-goody. Daphne's a selfish brat, that's what she is, admit it."

"Shush, here she comes."

By the dimmest light that still enabled her to see, Lucy began to write.

Dearest Adam,

*I love your plans. I want to go to Massachu-
setts with you and help with anything you wish to
do in any way I can.*

*I wouldn't want Mama and Papa to know
this—they try so hard to give us interesting and
cultured lives in spite of limited resources and of
living in this little rural community. But Adam, I
will love being near a real city! Sally and Daphne
are very vocal about their desire to escape but I've
never said so, or maybe even so much thought it.
Now that I do think about it, I'm so excited and
eager. You know I would be happy to be with you
anywhere but what you describe is wonderfully
appealing to me. I want to see and hear the symphony! All the things I've only read about and
heard about. I'll love meeting different people and
hearing different ideas and points of view.*

*I want a change, a challenge. Lyda likes North
Carolina awfully well. She says Wilmington is
very similar but just a little different from South
Carolina and she enjoys that. She says meeting
and becoming friends with a whole crowd of new
people has been fun and stimulating. I'll like it
too. Don't worry about that for a moment.*

*Of course I'll like your family. They produced
you! They need no further credentials. As for my
family, I've never known Mama and Papa to make*

a serious misjudgment of a person. They will give us their blessing. I know they will.

My only real concern is poor Tom. I have treated him badly and I do hate that. Now I'm going to admit the truth to you, Adam, I am not concerned about Alicia. She doesn't deserve you! Besides, we can't build our lives on mistakes. We found each other. That must be a miracle of sorts.

Until Saturday, all my love,

—Lucy

* * *

Saturday dawned hot and humid. The atmosphere over Ashton was leaden. Sisters and servants moved slowly through the morning chores, spirits lowered by the unrelenting, heavy heat.

Lucy walked with Jenny down the hard clay path to the rural mailbox that stood on the edge of the Willoughby property. Nothing for her—nothing since Tuesday. What could be wrong? She felt ill with tension and anxiety.

"What is it, Lucy?" Jenny asked. "Do you feel sick?"

"We should have a telephone like normal folks," Lucy snapped. Lucy who never snapped, who was always patient and kind.

The day dragged on.

Mama drew Sally aside. "You'd better tell me

exactly what's going on with Lucy. Obviously it's more than I realized."

So it was that Mama, Sally and Lucy converged upon the front door when, just at dusk as a breeze at last lightened the heavy atmosphere, a motorcar drove up. Captain Clayton sprang out and hurried to the door. At the sight of his stricken face, Lucy turned cold with fear, nausea rising in her throat.

"Lucy, Mrs. Willoughby, I have the most terrible news. May we sit down?"

"No, no, tell me now, quickly." Lucy gripped his arm. "What's happened?"

"Adam became ill on the parade ground Monday. He resisted going to the infirmary until yesterday when he collapsed in the mess hall. It's that terrible Spanish influenza. He's asking for you, Lucy, he's losing ground fast. Will you come?"

Lucy walked straight out the door. Papa appeared at her side. He had his hat. He took her arm. They got into the car quickly. The captain jumped in beside them and they roared down the red clay road toward Camp Jackson.

"I've arranged things," the captain said, never taking his eyes from the road or losing speed. "The head physician is a classmate of mine, not regular Army, willing to bend the rules. Adam's in isolation, you can wear a mask. This thing is not as contagious as people think, if precautions are taken."

"It doesn't matter. I'm not afraid," Lucy said.

"Hurry." Papa had his arm around her. He didn't speak—Papa silent!

Adam, Adam, save him God, spare him.

They stopped. They must be there. She ran up the steps, the Captain running beside her.

"Hurry, hurry," she said as the doctor tied on her mask and slipped some kind of gown over her dress.

While the doctor was tying her mask, Papa walked by. Throwing his hat aside he strode through the swinging door.

Lucy and the doctor hurried behind him. Papa had pulled a curtain back and was bending over a hospital bed speaking quickly and urgently.

"Adam, my boy, fight hard. Mrs. Willoughby and I like you. We approve of you for our Lucy. We want you to know that, son."

When Lucy rushed up, Papa and the doctor stepped out of the room.

"Adam," she pushed the mask from her face. "I'm here. I love you. I love you."

His eyes opened—that startling blue. They locked with hers. Dear God. She thought her heart would burst.

"Lucy, my Lucy, don't forget me." His voice was a hoarse whisper.

"Don't leave me—don't." She bent and kissed him on his burning forehead. His eyes closed. His breath came in uneven rasps.

Let him live! Please, God, let him live. I'll give him

up, Alicia can have him—anything, anything. Oh please take me instead.

She grasped his hot hand and brought it to her lips.

Again his eyes opened, locked with hers.

"Lucy, Lucy—love you so—don't forget—never—

His rasping breath stopped.

"Adam! Adam!" She put her head down on his chest—his chest, hot, hot through the hospital shirt, but still, oh so still!

The doctor was beside her. "Step out now, Miss Willoughby, it's over."

"No, no."

But he put a firm arm about her shoulders and guided her out.

When she saw Papa, waiting just outside the door, the tears came. They rolled down her cheeks but she made no sound. Papa stepped up and enfolded her in his arms. He held her tightly against his chest. He rested his cheek against her hair.

"He knew me, I saw his eyes. He looked straight at me. He spoke to me."

The captain was saying he had to stay, he had a sergeant standing by to drive them home.

"Sit in the back seat with your father, Lucy. Thank God we made it. He deserved to have his last wish. He deserved everything. He was a treasure while we had him, Lucy."

Papa held her while she cried, still quietly. She couldn't speak. She couldn't think. She couldn't really feel, yet.

Papa said nothing for what seemed a long time. Then he held her away from him, keeping only her hands tightly in his.

"Look at me, Lucy."

She looked. His sharp brown eyes glowing through the deepening dusk locked with hers so forcibly that the effect was hypnotic.

"Now listen carefully. If you forget every other word I've spoken, I want you to remember what I am saying to you now.

"This overwhelming grief will pass. It always does. You've known a wonderful romantic love. This is one of life's blessings, given to only a few. But most blessings, dear daughter, come with a high price tag. Life is hard, very hard. Life's terrible blows must be met head on. You must never surrender to them. You must keep standing and rise up from whatever is dealt you and grasp with both hands the good things in life that remain. This is the only life we have and we must live it well.

"Seize the moments, savor every beautiful sight or sound or taste or human being that comes your way. And many will. You can't imagine that now, my girl, but you must simply trust me on this. Satisfactions, joys lie ahead.

"But for now we won't look ahead and you must try not to look back. The way we'll get through this is moment by moment, day by day. Your mother and your sisters and I are with you. That's what families are for. You'll get through this like the thoroughbred you are. Oh, I know you girls laugh at what you call my ancestor worship. But you'll see that courage and grace and the instinct to behave well are bred into your very bones and marrow. Ladies and gentlemen rise to whatever is required of them and you will do so now."

"Let's wake up now! Open those eyes. It's lunch time! All the others have begun. Dr. Reynolds has said a lovely blessing."

She is enraged. In her mind's eye she had almost seen his face. She had felt his presence. She was remembering, remembering. Oh, why can she not be left in peace?

She must be inside, must have dozed while they rolled her chair from the shade of the tree.

She opens her eyes as slowly as possible. She dreads the sight of the communal dining room, loathes the sound of this nurse's voice.

She wishes the place would employ mutes. Where do these women come from?—So officious, so stupid, such common voices.

She forgets which meal this is, perhaps lunch?

Ah, then she will have a "rest period." Back in infancy—some patronizing treatment, same schedule.

Well, the rest period suits her right down to the ground. She wants to rest. She wants to remember. She wants to remember Him. She will live again and then again those weeks with Him.

But when at last she is stretched on her bed in a darkened, quiet room, it's not His face she sees. She sees her sisters—her sisters—how they'd quarreled and scapped but how they loved one another. All gone now—only nieces and nephews left.

There is just nothing in this world like a sister. Eyes closed, she can be with them again—with Sally. Yes, Sally.

Sally

Ashton Plantation, September 1, 1918

SALLY HEARD CRAWFORD'S FORD RATTLING into the back entrance of Ashton just as the big grandfather clock struck five.

So he was on time, for once.

She dashed down the stairs and out the door. He got out from behind the wheel just as Papa strolled around the corner from the front yard. Crawford paused.

"How do you do, Sir?"

"Good evening, Crawford." Papa lifted his Panama hat.

How did Papa manage to convey such coldness while being so polite?

Crawford took off his army cap with one hand and extended the other to her, giving her a chaste peck on the cheek.

"Let's take a stroll in Mrs. Willoughby's beautiful flower garden," he said, "while we still have some light."

Papa's expression turned even colder but he proceeded on into the house.

As soon as they were out of sight of the house, Crawford sank down on the garden bench. He pulled her onto his lap, held her tightly and kissed her hard on the mouth.

Sally laughed and snuggled closer. If Papa could see this, he would finally burst that blood vessel that throbbed on his forehead when he was in a temper.

Oh, why couldn't she get Papa out of her mind? She was *going* to banish him from her thoughts, absolutely she was going to.

Crawford lit a cigarette, passed it from his lips to hers. He'd taught her how to inhale and she was growing quite fond of the habit. He gave her a squeeze, allowing his hand to wander a bit, as he was inclined to do lately. She pulled herself up straight immediately, and he laughed.

She loved how he was always laughing.

"Listen, Sally, my leave begins October first. We've got to get some invitations out and get this marriage thing done. October second is a Saturday, that should be the day. Talk to your mother. Mine can hardly wait to turn me over to you."

"Crawford, we're just all so sad for Lucy. Adam's death has taken the wind out of my sails when it comes to my own happiness."

"That's gone on long enough. It's over. Think of poor Tom Thornton—that's who I'm sorry for, you never saw such a crushed fellow."

"I'll talk to Mama tonight. We'll write the notes. Since it's family only, we can arrange things by October second, I know we can."

He pulled out his slim silver flask. "I'll drink to that." Then he threw back his handsome head and took a long swallow.

He was so *very* handsome, eyes as dark as hers and Papa's but lazy, with eyelashes like a girl's. He'd grown a mustache, as black as Papa's used to be, that tickled when he kissed her.

"Put that flask away right now. Papa would die."

He laughed again and took another long pull before she insisted that they go inside to the parlor.

* * *

October second arrived, a breathtakingly beautiful day, crisp air, bright sun. It was to be a noon wedding so she and Crawford could drive to Flat Rock by nightfall to begin their brief honeymoon. One of the Carsworth cousins had provided a vacation home in the mountains for the week.

"Sally, you look so lovely," Lucy said. She'd been steadfastly cheerful all month. Sally knew she was determined not to let her own sorrow cloud Sally's happiness.

"Lucy, I always wanted to be tall and beautiful like you."

"You may not be tall, but Papa's right, you're a pocket Venus with all that beautiful golden hair."

"Papa." Sally sighed. "Either he's wonderful and making us feel wonderful too, or he's in a rage."

"Sally, don't start on that. He's downstairs waiting in that fine car Mrs. Bellinger insisted on lending us. That fancy Joseph who works for them is driving. You'll feel like a Broadway star."

Lyda's dress had been taken in for Sally, and she was wearing Mama's tulle veil. She pinched her cheeks, and looked in the mirror. For all her protests, she was quite pleased with her looks. But she would certainly try a little discreet make-up when she escaped Ashton. Everyone else did.

But now—now it was time for her to join Papa for the last ride she would ever take as Sally Willoughby. Her heart was beating fast. To tell the truth, she was a little frightened. She had opposed Mama and Papa and stood her ground against their advice in this, the most important decision of her life. Well it was done. She lifted her chin and sailed out into the sunlight and down the outdoor floating stairway of Ashton.

"Sally," Papa said when she had settled in the seat beside him, "it's not too late to change your mind. If you have the slightest reservation, I'll take care of everything and we'll call this off."

"Papa." Her eyes filled with tears. "No."

He took her hand. "It's all right, Sally. If you're quite sure, then your mother and your sisters and I are all behind you. Remember, Ashton and your family are always right here."

He kissed her cheek just as they pulled up in front of the little country church.

* * *

After the ceremony, the families returned to Ashton for lunch. Coastal accents filled the old parlor. The Carsworth cousins exuded that special Charleston charm, a combination of bone-deep self-assurance and effortless, perfect manners.

Crawford's mother and his older sister, Eloise, were of an entirely different stripe. Formal, humorless, plain.

"Well, they're Pendletons," Mama had explained. "A fine old Charleston family but they've always produced those plain, stern women and those men who see to trust funds and college endowments and accounts and such, never anyone lively enough to become even an Episcopal rector, they behave like Methodists. I can't imagine why Al married poor Vivien—can you, Colonel?"

"She had a considerable nest egg," Papa said. "That's what accountants are good for, you know, and Al had finished off what was left of his branch of the Carsworth money by the time he was twenty-five. Most unfortunate that the daughter so closely resembles her mother."

Sally had scarcely listened. She was hurrying

somewhere at the time. She was always in a hurry. Right now on October 2, 1918, she was in a hurry to head off in that model-T with her husband. Her *husband*!

"Crawford, maybe it's time to change into our traveling clothes and leave. Are you ready?"

"Mrs. Carsworth, you can't imagine how ready. Let's go."

She opens her eyes—cautiously, only halfway. Ah, she is alone, it is quiet, peaceful. The sun is still warming her sore old bones but it is gentled by the leaves of the sheltering tree. Is it afternoon?

She thinks of Sally—her Sally getting ready to leave Ashton with Crawford. She feels again that tug of loss, the loss of Sally. Having Sally near was such a comfort once she knew she would never have Adam. She closes her eyes. She will think of Sally.

But no, it is Daphne who appears in her mind's eye, poor Daphne, so pretty, so restless, so discontent.

Daphne

DAPHNE STOOD AT THE BOTTOM of the curving wooden stairway that led from the second floor of the old plantation house down to the lawn below. She was waiting for Sally and Crawford to appear. But they were taking so long she was bored, and besides it was growing uncomfortably hot in the sun.

Furthermore she was stuffed. Just because it was a noon wedding did they have to have all that old-fashioned plantation food? The huge old dining room table should have collapsed under its load—a whole ham, a leg of lamb, a roasted turkey, potato soufflé, rice with gravy, and green beans, squash, okra, tomatoes, all from Papa's garden and canned last summer. On a separate table were the breads—cornbread, biscuits, Josephine's light-as-air rolls. And then the dessert table! Apple, blueberry, and lemon meringue pies, cakes of all sorts along with the beautiful white-iced bride's cake and chocolate-iced groom's cake. Mama had made those herself.

If they didn't come soon people might begin to

faint, especially those Charleston men and even several of the women. She'd seen them sneaking to the porches for swigs from the flasks the men carried.

"Here they come," a Charleston voice said behind her. "Get ready."

Sally and Crawford ran out; she in a smart green traveling suit and cloche hat; he resplendent in his dress uniform, captain's bars gleaming on his shoulders.

Sally paused at the top of the steps. She looked over the noisy crowd, raised her arm and tossed her bridal bouquet straight at Lucy.

Of course, always Lucy. Neither Sally nor Lucy ever seemed to know she was alive except when she managed to do something to annoy Sally—which was just about everything she did. At least, thank heavens, Sally would be out of the way. Of course, Lucy was still around.

It just wasn't fair. First Lyda, then Sally and Lucy taking all Mama's time and Papa's interest. She was left with dull Mary, not to mention Jenny, rotten, spoiled, baby Jenny.

I'm getting away from here. If only we weren't so poor!

Just then she felt large firm hands at either side of her slender waist.

"And which Miss Willoughby is this? Crawford's kept you hidden from us, the cad."

Mama and Papa were nowhere in sight. She

leaned back toward the voice, turned and smiled. "I'm Daphne."

"Well, I'm Eddie, Crawford's cousin, and it's certainly a pleasure to meet you. How about giving me a tour of the neighborhood? That's my car over there." His hands were still on her waist, and she was smiling.

"Daphne!" It was Papa's voice. Eddie's hands dropped instantly and he sprang back.

"Go help your mother bid goodbye to our guests." He turned to Eddie, "Good day, sir."

Oh, she never got to have any fun. She glanced around and saw Tom Thornton easing over toward Lucy. He'd scarcely taken his eyes off her throughout the ceremony and reception, poor thing. Now if only someone like that divine, handsome Adam would come around again and notice *her*. But she was too young for the soldiers and the local boys were all boring. And poor.

* * *

The next day Lucy left with Lyda and James for a visit to Wilmington. A change of scene would be good for her, Papa decreed.

And for me, Daphne sighed. Maybe, just maybe, she could be the center of attention for once.

That night she took a long time arranging her hair and looked carefully through Lucy's chest of drawers. She found a blouse that she thought would fit her, and beneath the folded, scented camisoles, the letters she'd brought in to Lucy that she knew were from Adam. She sank down on the floor and started reading. Lucy and Sally might think she didn't know what was going on, but she'd been in the parlor when Adam came that Saturday morning and looked at Lucy as if he could swallow her whole. She'd seen Sally and Lucy leave with that captain and his wife and Adam. She'd seen Lucy sneaking out those Sundays. She'd been dying to tell Mama what goody-goody Lucy was up to, but whenever she had told Mama anything about her sisters, Mama never thanked her, just said she should concentrate on what she was doing, not the others.

Thinking about Mama took some of the pleasure from her interesting investigation. And Papa, too. He was never pleased with her. Could she help it if she wasn't a good student? She simply didn't have the family fascination with books and ideas. She liked her piano and singing lessons better than attending Ellerton Academy.

She heard Mama welcoming Ned, who was calling for Mary, and she hurried to complete her toilette.

Lucy's blouse was a nice fit. *It looks better on me than it does on skinny Lucy.*

She tucked it in tightly to emphasize her curves. She'd shortened a black taffeta skirt of Sally's so that her ankles were thoroughly exposed. A wide red sash that happened to be her own completed her costume. She shook a few curls loose, pinched her cheeks and was quite satisfied with the result of her efforts.

Joe Thornton and Bill Tiller had ridden their horses over. She'd grown up with both boys and was tired of their company, but it was fun to tease them into a competition for her attention. She flounced into the parlor, tossing her curls as her swains rose and rushed to be first at her side. Just then Mary walked in with a boy Daphne had never seen before. "This is Tim Nettles from Rembert," she said. "This is my sister Daphne. Tim coaches hockey at the Academy. All of us teachers are hoping he'll study to be one, too, we need more men to help us with those boisterous boys."

He looked at least eighteen!

Daphne turned her blue eyes and dimpling smile on Tim, and within a few minutes, he was on the piano bench singing duets with her while she played the tunes.

When Papa said, "It's time the younger gentlemen were leaving," Tim lingered behind, grasping her hand the moment the others headed down the steps.

"Miss Daphne, may I call again? May I write you?" She looked up at him, raising her head very slowly and then lifting her long lashes still more slowly.

"Oh, please do."

When she turned to say goodnight to Mama she received an icy look and a cool goodnight in return. Oh, well. It was worth it. She was bored silly.

Sally

CRAWFORD HAD RECEIVED ORDERS TRANSFERRING him from Camp Jackson to Camp Bragg. And so, after only a week, the bride and groom drove straight from the mountains of North Carolina to the flatlands of Fayetteville.

"Why on earth send me to Camp Bragg?" Crawford had grumbled. "It's France I've been training for."

He wanted to fight—marry Sally, then go right into battle. He seldom made long-range plans but he had pursued those two goals relentlessly.

Sally loved the army post. The Officers' Club was always full of young men—men from all over the United States. The sprinkling of wives who accompanied them represented all spectrums of society. It was Sally's first glimpse of the big world, just what she'd been longing for. She had her hair cut, she shortened her skirts. She couldn't, after all, quite bring herself to try any face painting, but fortunately she didn't really need it yet.

If some of her new friends occasionally struck her as not quite ladies and gentlemen, she stifled the thought. She aimed to move beyond the narrow confines of the old-fashioned standards in which she'd been raised. She smoked, she sipped an occasional highball, she danced with abandon and laughed more loudly and more often than she had ever done before, with Crawford egging her on. They were the most sought-after couple at the base—he so handsome, she so charming, both such fun to be with. If she sometimes arrived home with a husband walking unsteadily and slurring his words a bit, so what? She loved their time at Camp Bragg and hated to see it end. As it happened, Sally and Crawford were at the Officers' Club when they heard about the Armistice. Amid the cheers surrounding them, Crawford turned to Sally, his dark face flushed.

"My God, I've spent all this time training and don't get to fight! Not even one battle, just shuffling around the hottest places in the Carolinas."

"But, darling, you're safe. I didn't say it but I was so, so worried about you. The way you ride and hurtle over those high jumps—the way you swim halfway into the Atlantic—heavens—just the way you whiz around curves in your automobile scares me half to death. Now at least I won't have to worry about you being wounded or gassed or even killed!"

As if he hadn't heard her, he pressed on. "Next to marrying you, I've wanted to cross the ocean and get in that war more than anything. Now I've missed my chance forever."

Crawford sank his head into his hands while the cheers resounded around him.

Many years later the time would come when Sally, too, thought Crawford had missed what he might have done best. Physical courage, physical ability, daring—those were Crawford's assets. He should have finished his life on a battlefield, as a hero.

* * *

The severance check that came with Crawford's discharge lifted both their spirits. They drove to Wilmington for a visit with Lyda.

She and Sally talked nonstop—the Willoughby sisters, their husbands agreed, could easily talk and listen at the same time. Sally loved being with Lyda. Tears stung her eyes when it was time to head toward Charleston.

"You're mighty quiet, Miss Sal," Crawford said, after they had driven a considerable time in silence. "Did you injure your vocal cords? I wouldn't be surprised."

"Crawford, I've got something to tell you." She paused. He waited.

"Come on, Sally, spit it out, whatever it is."

"Well, I was pretty sure about it but since I've talked to Lyda I'm positive." She took a deep breath, "Crawford, I'm going to have a baby."

"Oh, my God!"

The car swerved out of control for a second. Sally put her head in her hands and sobbed; Crawford pulled over to the shoulder of the highway and put his arms around her.

"Darling, I didn't mean it like it came out. I'm just surprised. It'll be wonderful to have any baby that's yours."

"But the timing is just terrible. Now we won't have any chance at all of going to Atlanta."

Sally had been pressing Crawford to contact his Atlanta relatives about a job. She dreaded settling down in South Carolina, and although Charleston was her favorite place in the whole state, a closer acquaintance with Mrs. Carsworth and Eloise had disabused her of any desire to live there.

Sally arrived at the Carsworth home on Tradd Street dispirited and beginning to feel ill every morning.

Only a small portion of the house faced onto the street. Like most Charleston town houses, this one went straight back and mostly up, with the entrance on the side.

Good heavens, it's in worse shape than Ashton.

Her spirits sank lower.

But her training from Mama and Papa kicked in, and she was steadfastly cheerful as she and Crawford settled in on the third floor.

"Crawford," she said when they were alone in the rooms that were to be theirs, "I thought the other floors were bad but this beats all. I suppose it was for children and mammies."

"I guess so. Poor Eloise has taken over my old room as a sitting room for herself. But the further away we are from those two, the better." His good manners required that he treat his mother and sister with unfailing courtesy, but his opinion was something else again.

Oscar Pendleton, his mother's brother and a bank president, provided a job. Before the baby's birth they managed to put together enough money to rent their own place. It was only a half-house on Franklin Street but it was on the south side of Broad Street which made it an acceptable place to live.

The owner, Mrs. Smythe, an old family friend, had turned the first floor of her home into a rental property when her husband died. She now existed on the income from this while living on the second story herself.

"Oh Crawford, everything will be so much better now. I love your friends, and their wives have taken me in so wonderfully. We can have people over and have fun again, just as soon as the baby's born and I can go out."

"Expecting" women remained in their houses as much as possible, at home only to other females or very close relatives. Sally felt like a prisoner but forced herself to behave properly nonetheless. Why give his dragon mother and sister something to hold against her?

Since she had to stay in anyway, Sally occupied herself arranging her first real home.

She had always had a fine sense of style and a flair that enabled her to take clothes passed down from older sisters and make adjustments and additions so that when she appeared in them she looked up-to-date and beautifully turned out.

Mrs. Carsworth allowed her to take her pick of the third floor furniture and then added a secretary and two tables that were of museum quality but, it so happened, had not yet been sold to any of the dealers who were always prowling Charleston for original Sheratons and Hepplewhites. Worn oriental rugs were plentiful even on the third floor, so Crawford left his old home with a car full of them.

A tiny room off the kitchen was provided for a servant. No Southerner of Sally's class even considered doing without household help, which ranked with food and shelter as an absolute necessity. Here again, Sally was fortunate. Addie, the teenaged granddaughter of Mrs. Carsworth's dour old retainer, begged to be allowed to leave her grandmother's dreary quarters and go to work for "Miss Sally" and "Mr. Crawford."

Addie turned out to be a kindred spirit. She and Sally laughed and chatted as they remade old draperies and scrubbed and painted the walls, forming a friendship that would last throughout Sally's lifetime.

As for Crawford's drinking, she tried not to worry but she did. There had been many times, indeed far too many, while they were still at Tradd Street, when he had arrived for their daily two o'clock dinner smelling of alcohol. Although he gave no sign of this indulgence, he must have been partaking of the silver flask, either at the bank or as he walked home. She mentioned it to him. He laughed it off. There were evenings, too, when he arrived home late from his afternoon at the bank, red-eyed and unsteady on his feet when he reached the house.

It *had* to be obvious to Mrs. Carsworth and Eloise. One evening the three women finally sat down to their light supper without him, and afterward settled into a strained wait in the parlor until he drifted in, listing heavily to one side and smiling confusedly.

"Please, Crawford, you must stop this," Sally said, upstairs in their room. "It's so terrible for you, bad for your career. It's so hard to see you this way—not yourself, slow and stupid and stumbling—not at *all* yourself."

"Yes, sure, Sally."

But his eyes were already closing.

The next day she approached Mrs. Carsworth

when she found her alone in the garden.

"I don't want to worry you, but I'm getting very anxious about Crawford's drinking. I think he's going to harm his health and certainly his work. Uncle Oscar must disapprove terribly. What can we do?"

Mrs. Carsworth turned a cold stare upon her.

"Crawford's health has never been strong. And now with a child on the way he's under a great deal of pressure."

Sally began to realize that she and her mother-in-law would never understand each other. She longed for her own articulate, forthright parents. But how could she even mention her worries to Mama and Papa considering their repeated warnings and heartfelt opposition to her marriage? Would it be disloyal to discuss the problem with Lucy, perhaps? She felt Addie's support and empathy daily but could never speak of it.

The good times still outweighed the bad, those times when Crawford ran up the steps at two o'clock sharp and swept her up and around, kissing her face and lips, laughing, making her laugh, making Addie smile as she served up their dinner. So the long hot summer days of her pregnancy passed.

On the good evenings Crawford would drive her to the Isle of Palms, where they would spread a quilt on the beach and eat a picnic supper while the fevered sun set and at last a cool moon and breeze lightened the air.

Crawford liked to swim before supper. When he emerged from behind a sand dune in his bathing suit, his slim, hard athletic body somehow reassured her. Surely, he was all right. He would dash into the ocean and swim so far so fast that she caught her breath with fright for him. She would take off her shoes and stockings and wade in the tepid water while she watched for his black head on the horizon.

He loves me, I love him, surely it's enough? He'll be all right?

* * *

Mama came to be with her when Dr. Jones decided that birth was imminent. She settled into the little guest room.

"Oh, Mama, it's wonderful to have you all to myself," Sally said. "I never have before."

"Dear Sally, you've said just what I've thought myself for all these years, oh, if only I could sometimes have my precious girls just one at a time." Mama opened her arms and Sally walked into them.

Addie and Mama turned the dressing room attached to the master bedroom into a nursery. Mama exercised all her charm on Mrs. Carsworth and Eloise. She gave every evidence of enjoying Crawford's company.

Dear Lord, just let him act properly while Mama's here.

And so he did as the first week passed in happy activity.

It was four o'clock on a burning August day when Mama, Addie and Sally were resting that Sally first felt pains that seemed regular.

Mama rose quickly, pulling on her dress, smoothing her hair.

"How close are the pains?"

"Well, not so close yet but I've felt strange all day and I thought they were beginning at dinner, so I didn't eat much."

"Good. Let's call Crawford so he can come home as soon as it's convenient, but we might wait a while on Dr. Jones."

"Mr. Carsworth hasn't returned from dinner." The secretary who worked with the trust officers answered the phone.

Sally suddenly felt quite ill. Crawford had left home before three o'clock.

"Please have him come home immediately when he arrives, Miss Jenkins. We think the time has come."

She didn't tell Mama. Mama didn't ask.

They walked about through the shaded but still stifling rooms. Mama fanned Sally's flushed face. Addie brought chilled lemonade and joined in the fanning. The pains came closer and harder. Sally phoned the bank again. Mr. Carsworth had neither called nor arrived.

Oh God, oh Crawford, how could he do this to her?

The sun was setting, the heavy air was mercifully lifting and it was long past Crawford's usual time to come home when Mama decided Dr. Jones should be called.

"Sally, tell him the pains are five minutes apart now and let's get his opinion. Things have changed since my day."

Dr. Jones and his nurse arrived before hard dark. While Addie assisted in the preparations in the large bedroom, Mama slipped to the telephone and called Mrs. Carsworth.

"Eloise, the baby is most certainly coming soon. I feel sure you and young Eloise will leave no stone unturned in locating Crawford. I'm counting upon you. Sally must not be further upset."

Four hours later came the baby, red and squalling, plump and female.

"Oh, Mama, a girl, oh, isn't she beautiful? Why did I ever, *ever* think I wanted a boy?"

Then the front door opened and they heard Crawford's unsteady steps.

Dr. Jones, who had known him all of his life, met him in the hallway.

"You're quite a bit too late, Crawford. Now pull yourself together, damn it! Throw water on your face, straighten up and get in there and act like a man. You're a father now!"

Crawford stumbled through the door but could only mutter regrets. He was beyond acting like a man—much less a father.

* * *

The baby was named Elizabeth for Mama, but Sally called her Liz right from the beginning.

Sally knew moments of peace, a peace that was close to happiness when she was nursing Liz or just holding and rocking her. But at all other times she felt as if a heavy stone were lodged in her chest.

She turned her face from Crawford, kept her door closed, tried to be her old self only when her young friends came by. Mama left as soon as she had settled in the baby nurse Dr. Jones sent over to help. Sally was supposed to stay in bed for a month, but when she got up a few days after the baby was born and began to pace about her room, Mama said nothing. She held Sally close when she said goodbye.

"Darling, you must come for a visit just as soon as Dr. Jones says you may travel. Liz will give us all so much pleasure."

Yes, oh yes, she would go to Ashton. She could hang on until it was time to go to Ashton.

If Mama and Crawford had any discussion of the disastrous evening, she didn't hear about it.

Then Lucy arrived, the very day Sally finally managed to rid herself of the complaining nursemaid. When Lucy stepped in the door, with Crawford behind her carrying her suitcase, Sally felt something loosen inside, she thrust Liz into Crawford's arms and herself into Lucy's. Then she broke into wracking, body-shaking sobs. When Lucy began to cry also, Crawford handed Liz to Addie and made his escape.

It all poured out, the anxious months with Mrs. Carsworth, the growing fear and helplessness, the terrible night of Liz's birth.

"Oh, Sally," Lucy said, "do you know that old proverb 'Beware of your heart's desire, lest you should get it?' You got yours and it's come to this. I didn't get mine and my heart's broken. It's a cliché but that's what it feels like, something broken inside me. Remember how we longed to be grown up? Who would ever, ever have thought it would be like this?"

* * *

Sally completely ignored the bed-rest order and got up every day, pacing around the small house, accompanied by Lucy who made no attempt to enforce the injunction. She cajoled Sally into her trousseau nightgowns and robes and into fixing her hair; otherwise she left her alone. Who knew better than Lucy the folly of direct opposition to Sally?

The sisters began to go out in the little back garden that was shared with Mrs. Smythe. After the punishing sun went down, they sat in yard chairs under the old banana tree and passed Liz from lap to lap. They reminisced about their childhood and gossiped about their sisters.

Mary seemed unable to choose between her two stodgy suitors, Lucy reported. Not much choice there anyway, they agreed.

"Daphne considers herself the reigning belle now that you're gone, Sally."

"And you've retired," Sally said. "The horrid little hypocrite really is awfully pretty."

"She is," Lucy said. "She's got those gorgeous golden curls and big eyes."

"Like yours," Sally said.

"Anyway," Lucy said, "the boys are back in the colleges now and she's determined to have her share—or more, rather. It delights her to completely eclipse poor Mary."

"I wonder what Mama and Papa really think about her?" Sally said. "They're pretty sharp, as you and I well know, but could they realize that she has that horrid trait of not only wanting to succeed herself but of being so pleased when others fail?"

"I don't know, she's their child, they may not realize. But I tell you who'll put her in her place one of these days—our Jenny. She's such a feisty girl, so like you, bright and pretty."

The sisters sat in companionable silence for a while.

"Alicia got married last week," Lucy said, "a hurry-up thing to a man she met at Camp Jackson. He's a West Pointer and regular army, so they'll be moving on soon. I certainly hope so."

"She's probably pregnant, the bitch." Sally's time

as an army wife had enlarged her vocabulary.

"I'm ashamed of it, but I despise her," Lucy said. "I loathe the way she went around Columbia acting bereaved when Adam died. It was so horrid, so unnecessary. She could have just stayed quiet."

"I *bet* she's pregnant, Adam was too much of a gentleman ever, ever to say—even to you—but I would bet you anything that's how she got that ring out of him, sleeping with him, then making him feel guilty."

Lucy said nothing, which let Sally know she agreed.

Just then Mrs. Smythe emerged from the upstairs rooms that comprised her part of the old home, followed by her cook, who was carrying a tray with a pitcher of lemonade and platter of cookies.

Lucy smiled. "Oh, how lovely, Mrs. Smythe. Please take my chair, I'll pull up another. What a treat." She bustled about arranging things.

Sally knew Mrs. Smythe must be scandalized that she was up—and outside—with a three-week-old baby. But she also surmised the truth—that she warmly liked Sally and thoroughly disliked Mrs. Carsworth, her presumed friend. She was most likely aware of Sally's problems. They were known, if unacknowledged, all over Charleston.

* * *

It was very hard to part with Lucy but Sally knew Mama and Papa needed her help at home. Just before her departure, Sally ventured, "Is Tom coming around again, now?"

"He is, Sally, bless his heart. In a way he's a comfort to me, but I don't know. I just can't get Adam out of my mind. I don't want to, I want to see his face in my mind's eye. I can almost feel his arms and lips. I just don't want to let it go."

"You'll have to, you know. It's wrong. You need a home, a child. You're full of love, you've got to use it."

So the sisters parted, with advice flowing from Sally to Lucy instead of the other way around.

* * *

Toward Crawford, Sally felt frozen. She could barely look at him, she flinched from his touch. He appeared promptly each evening, sober if slightly haggard, as soon as he was free from the bank. Mrs. Carsworth and Eloise came to call once a week, occasionally bearing some heavy piece of old Carsworth silver for the infant but never showing any real enthusiasm.

Are they made of stone?

Am I turning to stone like them?

When Liz was six weeks old, Dr. Jones declared that she and Sally might take the train to Ellerton. Ashton! Sally's spirits rose. She was almost like her old self as she and Addie dashed about getting ready and finally departed, loaded with luggage, mostly for Liz.

The old house worked its magic. Sally revived. Mama and Papa actually argued over who was to hold Liz during the brief hour in late afternoon when her sunny disposition turned cranky. Mary was teaching first grade in the little country school that served the former plantations and whatever children drifted in and out from migrant laborers. Negroes were, of course, in another school, "probably a better school," Papa grumbled. "Could hardly be worse than the white school except for you, Mary. The races, not combining forces, what folly." Papa had very advanced ideas. He had predicted that machines would fly in the sky long before automobiles had been developed. His eccentricity was tolerated.

Jenny devoted herself to Liz, while Lucy, who gave piano lessons in addition to her real job as Mama's chief assistant, simply basked in the pleasure of being with Sally. They stayed in their old room together with Liz. Lucy jumped up at the baby's slightest whimper so that Sally might sleep.

Then a letter came from Crawford. The Carsworth cousin had given him use of his Flat Rock cottage again. Uncle Oscar had said he might have the week off. He was coming for Sally and Liz and Addie, he would arrive early Saturday and they would drive straight on to the mountains.

"I'm not going. I'm happy here, at peace. I can't leave yet."

But apparently Papa had heard from Crawford also. He invited Sally outside for a stroll.

"You must go with him, Sally, he's your husband. You're duty bound to go the extra mile. Try to forgive him, for Liz's sake. Open your heart, make a fresh start. But remember we are here. As long as it stands, Ashton is your home. You may always come here when you need to, or simply wish to."

So, she left with Crawford, luggage strapped everywhere, Addie holding Liz in the back seat, Sally, stone-faced, beside her husband.

She was truly exhausted when, at almost midnight, they reached their destination. She nursed the groggy baby and went straight to bed, her back firmly to Crawford.

But the next morning her spirits rose. The air was crisp, the sunshine shone brilliantly on the reds and golds of the turning leaves. She took a long walk. She felt young. She felt well. Crawford went to hit a few golf balls while Addie settled them in.

Crawford returned with armloads of groceries and a box lunch for them all. "Miss Sally, I drew you a warm bath," Addie said. "I'll take Miss Liz for a walk in her carriage, we'll spend the afternoon. She's good and full up with your milk. You rest."

The bath did feel good. She lingered, relaxing, then she toweled off, slipped on a robe and stretched out, her eyes on the brilliant leaves just outside the window.

There was no knock, but she heard the door open. Crawford was standing in the doorway, his shirt open halfway down his tanned chest, his black hair falling across his forehead, the chiseled face almost perfect, like the old days. She looked up and met his eyes, looked at him steadily for the first time since that awful night.

"Sally." His voice was a hoarse whisper. He moved across the room with his graceful stride, holding her eyes with his. She watched the light kindle inside those beautiful eyes, now clear and shining.

"I love you, I love you." He sank to his knees beside the bed, his eyes still holding hers. "For God's sake, Sally, give me another chance." Tears came to his eyes and he buried his face in her neck. She lay very still for a moment as she felt his hot breath, his warm lips. Then she lifted her hand and put it on his dark head. They stayed immobile for what seemed a long time. He kissed her neck. She didn't move, but let her hand stay tangled in his hair. His lips moved up to her chin, her cheek, her lips. Gently, tenderly he closed his mouth on hers. Her breathing quickened and he bent closer until his pounding heart was beating against hers. She felt his stroking hand outside her silken trousseau robe. She stirred and kissed him back. His hand reached inside the robe and drew her up into his arms. She gave up the struggle and returned his embraces as all the old feelings poured back.

The week that followed would stay with her for

a lifetime. When she later wondered why she had stuck with him, why she had strived and struggled against such odds, she would remember the golden week at Flat Rock, better than their honeymoon, better than their courtship or all the male attention she would ever know before or after Crawford. Yes, they were golden days with Liz plump and sweet and good. Addie beaming as she rolled Liz away each day and left her alone with Crawford. Crawford, handsome, amusing, ardent; she loving him again, or loving him still.

* * *

Back in Charleston, Sally's love for the old city revived as well. She flung herself into the social whirl that began every fall. A Carsworth was always welcome everywhere and her zest, energy, and humor enlivened any gathering.

Liz was such a good baby, Addie was always there. It was very much like their time at Camp Bragg, except that here there were ladies and gentlemen only, to the last and least of them.

Ah, but the drinking. She tried not to watch Crawford too closely but she knew his abstinence was not total. She could detect even one drink now. She no longer drank at all herself, but she resumed the cigarettes she loved.

It was the morning of the St. Cecilia Ball, which always took place on the third Thursday in January, that she first felt the nausea. She recognized it this time immediately.

Oh no, surely not. It couldn't be. She would wait and see. But it was, of course it was. Oh dear God, what would they do? The little house—Crawford—he couldn't stand up to pressure. What would she do?

She waited a few weeks, then told him. He turned ashen. "You can't be," he said. Nursing mothers don't conceive."

She cried just as she had the last time, but now he gave no comfort. He simply paced about their bedroom, muttering oaths under his breath.

"Well *you're* supposed to see that it doesn't happen. Lyda said so, everyone says so, what do I know about such things? She—."

He whirled on her. "So, it's my fault as usual, every goddamned thing that goes wrong is my fault!"

It was a bad quarrel, the worst they'd ever had and over a baby, a poor precious baby who was entitled to be wanted and welcomed.

Crawford's drinking accelerated. Sally moved through the routines of her life but the zest was gone. Only Addie was there to help. She brought Sally weak sweet tea and soda crackers. Once Sally broke down and cried at her kindness. The little black girl's arms came around her.

"Oh Addie, you're such a comfort. What would I do without you?"

This time Mama didn't come for the birth and wouldn't let Lucy come.

"Sally, it will perhaps be best if Crawford knows that you are entirely dependent upon him. Of course, I'll come right down if things don't go well. Isn't it wonderful that we have a telephone at last?"

So they managed and another girl arrived in September, not as plump and placid as Liz. "A crying baby," Mama said. "Some are just like that, their little digestive or nervous systems on edge somehow. Be patient Sally, wait and see, she'll be your pride and joy one of these days."

They named the infant Eloise, for Crawford's mother, but she was always called Ellie.

Charleston, 1923

Sally was sitting in Mrs. Smythe's garden, watching her little girls push their doll carriages, on a late hot summer morning, when Uncle Oscar came to call.

Addie opened the back door for him. "Miss Sally, it's Mr. Pendleton." She sounded as if she were announcing the King of England.

"Why, Uncle Oscar, what a nice surprise." He kissed her cheek as she rose to greet him.

"Lovely little girls." He looked ill at ease, but then he always did. "Perhaps your nursemaid...?"

"Of course. Sit here under the tree, Uncle Oscar.

Addie, will you please go ahead and give the girls their lunch?"

She sat down beside him and forced herself to wait in silence.

He looked directly at her.

"This is very distressing to me, Sally." Indeed he looked distressed and considerably upset at the task that lay before him.

"Crawford's problem—his drinking problem, that is—has gotten out of hand. He's to take a month off without salary. At the end of that time, if he's fit to return, we'll try again. His mother and sister have agreed to take him in. He needs nursing care. You must protect those babies of yours. Perhaps you could go to your parents? I could find a young clerk to sublet this house for a month or so. They're always complaining about a lack of places to live, this isn't New York I tell them, no room for ugly new housing." He cleared his throat and looked away.

Oh, no, oh no, oh no.

"It's kind of you to tell me yourself—and kinder still to give Crawford another chance. I'll do all I can to help him succeed when he returns to the bank."

He rose and kissed her again. "Very brave girl, lucky man to have you. Goodbye, my dear."

Uncle Oscar deposited Crawford in his mother's home. Dr. Jones had been called.

"Addie." Oh, this was hard. "I'll have to take you to your grandmother's. You need the rest, anyway. Hide away from them all or they'll put you to work. There's no way we can pay you this month."

"Miss Sally, what I make don't amount to anything. I like that house in the yard and those nice folks I stay with at Ashton. Y'all always have such good food, too, and the work ain't nothing but playing with my girls. Maggie was teaching me to make my own clothes when I was there before. I'm goin' with you."

Even in the face of Dr. Jones, Crawford's inert body, and Sally's flashing eyes, Mrs. Carsworth still refused to acknowledge the real problem.

"Certainly, I shall nurse my son back to health. His lungs have always been weak." Eloise followed her lead.

The idiots! No wonder Crawford was the way he was. He should have been raised by people like Mama and Papa who called a spade a spade, or a drunk a drunk—people who cared about the substance of things, not the facade. How she despised them. She was going home, going home to real people.

Ashton, Ashton, the thought of it sustained her. She'd go tomorrow. Mama, Lucy, Papa—she could stand it if she were there with them. She knew she could.

So began the nightmare years.

She wakes with a start. Has she been dreaming? She almost saw His face for just a moment. She closes her eyes again to recapture the moment. She's in a cloud of white tulle, drifting down the aisle of All Saint's Church. Papa—she's holding hard to Papa's arm. Will she see His face? No, no it's Tom, poor dear Tom she sees.

Lucy

Ashton, October 1923

LUCY WAS GETTING READY FOR HER WEDDING.

Sally was helping her into the cream satin dress Mama and Lyda had made from a Vogue pattern. It had a dropped waist and a daringly short skirt that showed her legs.

"Now let's do the veil," Sally said, impatient as always.

Oh, it was a comfort to have Sally here. Crawford was in Charleston with his family, ostensibly recovering from a bronchial infection but in fact drying out. Sally and her babies had been at Ashton for a month. Lucy was happy to have had this time with them, perhaps the last close time.

She caught Sally's hand and held it tightly to warm her own cold one. Their eyes met in the mirror, Lucy's wide with fear, Sally's stern with warning.

"It's going to be fine," Sally said. "Brides are always scared to death, aren't they, Lyda?"

Lyda, who probably could remember only eager anticipation on her wedding day, nonetheless said, "Oh, yes, Lucy, it'll be fine. Tom's such a good person. He'll be very gentle and considerate. You mustn't be afraid."

She thinks it's *that*. Lucy looked up and her eyes met Sally's again. Sally understood. She understood it all. How would she manage when Sally went back to Charleston? Next to *Him*, in all her life she had loved Sally most, even better than Mama or Papa.

"You look beautiful, Lucy," Sally said. "You really are the family beauty—I take back all those times I got so mad when Mama said that. You're so slim and such gorgeous blue eyes"—eyes now brimming with tears.

In her mind's eye, she saw *His* face. Oh, would it never end? What was she doing? Was she really going to spend the rest of her life with Thomas Addington Thornton III of Ellerton, South Carolina, just because he loved her and because her family was so close to his family and because she was growing older and life was moving on?

"Yes," Sally said, just as if she had read her mind. "You're going to be glad all the rest of your life that you've made this decision. We'll never have to worry about you again. Tom will see to that."

And in a way he did. Ellerton was nearby. She was close to her family and to his. His awkward embraces became skillful. His love made her feel safe. They became a team.

Tom taught mathematics and science at the local high school, so there was never enough money. But she was used to that and easily assumed her rightful position as a leader of the small, provincial community. Keeping their house, with only Dukie's daughter Tillie to help, proved job enough for a while. But from the first, Lucy longed for a baby. Dear Lord, send me a baby. Yes, a baby, oh, please a baby. Then she would be happy like Lyda, and the void inside her would be filled—she would never think of *Him* again.

* * *

"Lucy," Tom said, "if you're really sure you want me to, I'll just run by the barbecue for a few minutes so as not to disappoint mother and father. I still think Tillie should be here with you. You're too softhearted, letting her off every time she asks. That girl is supposed to have a job."

"Oh, go along, Tom. The quiet will do me good. I'll sit here in the swing and stir up a breeze for myself."

To tell the truth, she didn't feel too well—sort of unsettled and aching. It must be the heat—two more months to go before the joyfully awaited baby's birth. Everything was ready. Mama and Mary had been sewing and smocking the tiny layette Lucy and Tillie washed and ironed with such care. As soon as she realized a baby was on the way, Lucy felt a contentment she hadn't known since she was a young girl.

She was enjoying housework now that a baby would make it seem worth the effort. She was a good housekeeper like her mother. The few fine old pieces of furniture that the two families had been able to spare the young couple were shined to perfection, while the makeshift pieces were brightly covered to create a warm, welcoming home.

The baby, the baby. That was what she had been born for, this tiny creature would justify her life, give it the purpose it had lacked, give her back the zest that she'd lost on a long ago summer day much like this one. She knew women who complained about their pregnancies, and then their babies, once they came. She never understood that. She'd loved caring for her younger sisters. She would take such pleasure in caring for her very own child. Was it just a nurturing nature?

Often she felt out of tune with her contemporaries, especially when they acted cynical and bored. Lucy longed to be useful and needed, she longed for love. No, it was that she longed *to* love. Yes, loving someone deeply was best of all.

Suddenly, the discomfort became a sharp pain, running from middle to back. She bent over and started toward the front door. As she did, blood gushed from her body, staining her muslin dress and the cushions of the swing.

Oh, no, dear God, oh no. Help me, God. My baby, my baby.

"Tom, Tom!" But it was already too late. By the time Tom came home, well before Tillie, it was all over. Lucy was barely conscious. But she had reached the hall inside and was cradling the little female fetus who had never drawn a breath.

The months that followed were very bad, almost as bad as that other time after that other death. She would wake before dawn, cold with terror and despair. She would ease close to Tom and pray. *Help me, God. I can't make it through this day. I can't get up. I can't go on.*

But somehow she did. It was perhaps the quaint upbringing that saw her through. Abbotts and Willoughbys didn't stay in bed and cry. They stood and faced down the world outside and the demons within. So she got up, bathed, dressed, nausea rising in her throat. She moved in a haze of anguish but she moved. Each day a sister or Mama would come.

"Let's go now, Lucy. We'll take a little walk. I'll make a cup of tea. That'll make us both feel better."

"Come here," Tillie," Mama would scold. Get busy now and bring us some cookies to have with this tea. Now, you stick close to Miss Lucy and make yourself good company."

Tom was patient and kind, but his disappointment was obviously secondary to his concern about Lucy.

"We'll have more children," he said. "You'll see, Lucy. Things will be fine again. Please cheer up."

Lucy turned her face away. The desperate anguish she felt deepened when he touched her, became almost unbearable when she tried to respond to his forced cheerfulness. She felt her eyes begin to fill, and looked away. She would *not* become a weeping, self-pitying female. *Dear God, give me strength.* That was her constant prayer.

Always, as soon as Mama or the sisters left, the heavy blackness deepened. Was Tom part of the problem? Because only the company of the women seemed to give her a few moments of ease. She grew thin and pale. But Mama and the sisters persisted until at least some food and drink had been consumed each day. She struggled on.

One evening when the heavy heat had lifted and a hint of autumn was in the air, Lucy turned to Tom as soon as he came home before he could begin his strained heartiness.

"I need to get away from the house for a while. Would you mind, if I spend a week or two at Ashton?"

"Certainly not, sweetheart, I'll take you over tomorrow." And so he did.

Lucy found that just being in the old loved house and garden soothed her raging pain.

She and Papa took long walks each day as dusk fell.

"Come now, Lucy." Papa took her arm, forced her to walk fast, then faster. He talked about inconsequential things and she was not required to respond. One night she stopped his flow of words to whisper, "Oh, Papa what *is* wrong with me?"

He didn't really answer the question but he said with absolute assurance, "It will pass, Lucy. Hold on. 'This too shall pass', I promise you."

They would call it depression now. Drugs would be prescribed, specialists consulted. At that time, in that small place, Lucy had only her family. They stepped in and she survived. Slowly the heavy blanket of misery began to lift.

She went home to Ellerton and Tom. She turned toward him instead of away. He loved her and she would love him back—*she would, she would.*

She became pregnant. She began to live again instead of just existing but she was never quite the same. The Lucy who had belonged to Adam Stover was gone as surely as he was.

From the very beginning, the second pregnancy was different. She was nauseated early on. Then she became extremely well and she stayed that way. She walked regularly, ate just what Dr. Parlor suggested, drank milk every day. The sisters and her mother never flagged.

When Lucy protested that she was absorbing too much of their time, Mama said, "Why, darling, now you see the advantage of there being so many of us. Someone's always free. Whatever else is family for?"

It was decided that Jenny would spend several weeks with Lucy during the summer. She was a cheerful young woman and she helped the time to pass.

And so, it came to be that on a hot summer day, Thomas Addington Thornton IV arrived in the world, red and robust, delivered in the old four-poster bed that Mama had managed to spare, by Dr. Parlor, who had delivered Lucy. Thomas was a good baby and he grew into a good boy. There were no other babies, which was a great disappointment. But if any one child could incorporate the virtues of many, this one did.

Lucy was to look back on Thomas's baby years as the happiest of her married life. She would hurry home from her little social and civic engagements to be with him. He smiled at the sight of her face, laughed at the sound of her voice. She would cover his fat little body with kisses, then hug him tight and feel at peace.

Tom's obvious pride and pleasure added to her joy. Yes, it was joy that she felt, real happiness. So Papa had been right after all. *Of course*, Papa had been right!

Sally

T<small>HE TWO YEARS THAT FOLLOWED</small> Sally's return to Franklin Street were always blurred in her mind's eye. There were a few good months, then Crawford began coming home late at night, really late. He always smelled of alcohol but was usually ambulatory.

One evening he arrived in the company of two men who were more or less holding him up between them.

"S-sorry to be late, Sal. 'Fellas—meet m' wife'."

"Sit right here, Crawford." She took him firmly in hand and pressed him into the closest chair.

"Thank you," she said coldly as she turned and looked for the first time at his companions.

The largest one spoke up.

"I'm Jake O'Callahan, Miz Carsworth, and he," he pointed toward the other man, "he's Joe Jenkins."

Their faces were swarthy, their expressions furtive, their clothes ill-fitting, cheap.

"We're, ah, colleagues of Crawford," their spokesman continued, "pleased to meet ya."

They backed out the door.

Colleagues! These didn't look like trust officers to her. Her heart began to pound, her anxiety was becoming fright.

The mornings were now given over to whispered admonitions from her, empty reassurances from Crawford. He became haggard, dissipated looking, his handsome face puffy and pale. She wasn't sure he was ever entirely sober.

She didn't know where to turn for help. How could she burden her poor aging parents with her worries? Their admonitions and pleas were still fresh in her ears. But to give them their due, neither had ever uttered the hateful words, "I told you so." Lucy had been through an awful stillbirth and sad period and now, thank heavens, had just delivered a healthy son. Sally struggled on. Addie's understanding and silent support were all she had.

Then came the most terrible night of all.

Crawford got home—late, as usual, but alone and not as drunk as most nights.

"Sit down, Sally. We might as well get this over with now. I have something shocking that I've got to tell you."

"Keep your voice down. Addie may still be awake and we don't want to rouse the girls."

"There isn't any way to tell you but straight out—federal bank examiners are in here. They've found shortages in several of my trust accounts. As God is my witness, Sally, I haven't taken a penny. You know all too damn well we don't *have* an extra penny. It's those men, O'Callahan and Jenkins. They were always coming over just at closing time, bringing a bottle of bourbon. Of course I was drunk, they could have done anything. Oh God, Sally, I've ruined myself, I've ruined us all." He put his head in his hands and sobbed.

Her head swam.

"You mean you will be discharged?" Her voice shook.

"Worse, much worse—God, Sally, I've got to get a lawyer. I may go to jail."

* * *

A cousin—Mr. Legare, head of one of Charleston's oldest law firms—was summoned. He in turn called the best trial lawyer of his acquaintance, a category in which he had very few contacts. Sally and the girls left for Ashton, Papa himself having arrived to escort them. After all, he, too, was an attorney. After consulting with Mr. Legare and Mr. Witherspoon, the trial lawyer, Papa's face was the grimmest Sally had ever seen it.

Oh but surely, surely Papa can do something, Papa can always do something.

On the train to Ellerton, when Addie took the girls away, Papa tried to explain.

"If this were not a federal matter, Sally, we would have negotiating room. The Pendletons and Carsworths and our folks, too, could call in all our chits. Oscar could make up the money—it would half kill him but of course he would do it, and Crawford could walk free. But it's in federal courts, out of our hands, out of our sphere of influence. Those fellows, O'Callahan and Jenkins, have disappeared entirely, not that it matters. Those were Crawford's trust accounts from which the money is missing. He's got to go to trial, he may have to go to jail. Oscar can't stop any of it. It's the law."

Oh, God, oh my God—She felt dizzy, unable to breathe. "Papa—excuse me." She ran to the platform and gulped in the fresh air, holding tightly to the door handle. She saw Papa's anxious face in the glass. He had followed her.

They returned to their seats.

"There's nothing we can do about Crawford, my dear. You must think of yourself, and of your daughters. They'll be sheltered from the worst at Ashton. We're all with you, Sally—you're not alone." He took her hand. "Now just sit quietly. We will survive this."

Papa kept her hand in his for the rest of the trip.

* * *

The little girls settled in at Ashton. Mama and Jenny took over their care. They were kept busy, diverted. They were healthy and seemed happy.

Sally returned to Charleston. She put everything in her little house up for sale. Her friend Alice Perineaux stepped in to help, calling antique dealers, getting bids.

"There's no need to let yourself be cheated, Sally. Charleston antiques are in demand everywhere."

She sold Crawford's Ford, antique silver, Oriental rugs. She was in a frenzy to get rid of it all. Money! She must have money. Mrs. Smythe was kind, everyone was kind, but she could neither eat nor sleep nor rest.

"Selling your Sheraton secretary, the Pembroke tables?" Mrs. Carsworth's eyebrows rose with her voice.

"Yes—that is, unless *you* plan to pay the lawyers." Sally's voice was full of the scorn she felt.

Mrs. Carsworth sighed and turned away.

"Those dreadful men have caused this tragedy and now my Crawford is left holding the bag—he's too trusting, too kind-hearted, always has been."

Sally took a deep breath. She forced herself to speak calmly and quietly.

"I agree that Crawford is not a thief. However, the missing funds were *his* responsibility. He must take the consequences. The real victim is Uncle Oscar who will replace the money and who must continue to run a bank whose reputation is now tarnished."

Her mother-in-law simply left the room, closing the door more firmly than was necessary.

When everything had been sold, Sally took the money to Uncle Oscar himself, for deposit.

"Certainly, dear, I'll see that it earns the best interest possible."

Oscar Pendleton might be sickened nearly to death by what had happened to his precious bank, and he would certainly loathe the grand name of Carsworth to the end of his days, but he recognized courage when he encountered it.

The weeks passed. The families scraped together bail money that the local judge had set mercifully low. Crawford occasionally traveled by train to see Sally and his daughters. Only once did he permit himself to talk to Sally about his feelings or fears, although he never called them that.

"Oh Sal, I'll have to be in a cell with some common criminal—not a murderer, they're separated—but who knows what kind of thug. Locked up with a strange man, I guess for years, limited exercise, limited reading and writing material, never a minute of privacy, not seeing you, not being with you."

"You know I'm coming to see you as often as they allow it. I'll get there somehow."

"I'll see you through a *grill*. Jesus, to have to look at you from behind bars!"

"You've got to stand up to it, Crawford. We both have to. We can't crumble, *we must not crumble*. We'll hang on. Remember your daughters."

Crawford, through his lawyers, pled guilty. He

was sentenced to five years in the federal prison located in Atlanta

Ashton

"Papa, I'll have to get a job." Sally closed the
door to Papa's library and fixed him with the
haunted gaze she had acquired.

"Sit down, Sally. Let me see if I can help you sort
out your thoughts."

She lowered her eyes. Papa's gentleness had
brought the tears she was determined not to shed.

"I thought perhaps a secretarial course," he said.
"They have a good one right in Ellerton, connected
with the college. Only six weeks but very inten-
sive, shorthand and typing."

"Yes, that sounds best. Everyone has secretaries
now. I could stay week nights with Lucy. But my
girls?"

"The girls will be fine, Sally. Mary will take them
to school. Fortunately, she teaches first grade. She's
a fine teacher. They'll do well."

Mary had married—quietly, at Ashton, the qui-
etest of her long-time suitors, Ned Perkins. He had
moved into Mary's home to run the farm for Papa,
who was becoming frail, beginning now to seem as
old as he was.

Sally worked like a demon. She stayed late to
practice her typing, sailed through the preliminary

books, and into the advanced in three weeks. Between the work and the evenings at Lucy's and Tom's, some sort of healing of her wounded spirit began. Tom built up a big fire for the sisters. He urged one of his cigarettes on Sally, then left them to their talk. This time it was Thomas who went from lap to lap just as once it had been Liz.

"Sally," Lucy said, "do you realize that Mr. Kevin Worthington—whose large diamond Daphne is wearing so proudly—started out as Mary's beau?"

"I'd forgotten that. I've been in another world. What did that snake-in-the-grass do to poor Mary?"

"Took away the most exciting thing that had ever happened to her, that's all. Mary met him at a dance in Camden last winter. He was down with his horses and their trainer. He came courting Mary, but Daphne spotted the money and the glamour. She went after him and she got him. I'm glad Mary jumped in and married Ned right away. She's saved face, at least."

"I know Daphne could die at my disgrace," Sally said.

"What will those Kentucky people know about any of that? Besides, it is not *your* disgrace."

So the terrible weight that seemed to have settled on Sally's chest began to lift. There came an evening when she and Mama were having a late night cup of tea, when she finally let herself cry. She put her head in Mama's lap and sobbed until she was drained.

"Oh, Mama." She lifted her tear-stained face. "I'm so worried for my girls. This will ruin their lives."

"No, it will *not*. The bluest blood in South Carolina runs through their veins. The families will rally behind you and your girls. Crawford has ruined only himself. Always remember, your girls are also Abbotts and Willoughbys."

* * *

The very next day, as if her words had brought it to pass, Mama received a letter from her cousin, Edwin Abbott. Cousin Edwin's father had gone to Atlanta in the wake of the Civil War to seek his fortune in what was, by comparison to South Carolina, a land of opportunity. He'd started a real estate business, prospered, married an Atlantan, fathered Edwin, Jr. who was now president of Abbott Realtors. Edwin, Sr. had died, but not before instilling the proper values in his splendid son. Edwin, Jr. had been informed of the Carsworths' disaster. He was aware that this Carsworth fellow was married to an Abbott cousin. He was in a position to offer help to his cousin—that's what families were for. Blood was thicker than water, blood was everything.

He had his secretary call Ellerton Secretarial School, and when she reported that Sally Carsworth typed more words per minute than any previous graduate and took fast and near perfect shorthand, he dispatched a letter to the lovely older cousin he remembered from the annual Abbott reunions. He offered Sally a job. The salary named was breathtakingly generous. Furthermore, cousin Edwin wrote, he could place Sally and her daughters, if necessary, in a boarding house run by a lady and for ladies.

"Of course I'll go. But my girls and school?" Sally's voice shook a little.

"Perhaps," Mama said, "you should leave them here until the spring break. That way you can settle in and they can continue their work with Mary that's going so well. She thinks they're both very bright.

"But Mama, it's so much on you and Papa at your ages—and you have Daphne's wedding to work on right now."

"Nonsense, Jenny and Lucy love helping with the girls."

"Mama, are you sure?"

"Yes! Josephine feels useful looking after the girls' clothes and room. It's about all she can do now. Besides, Daphne is attending to her own wedding."

Addie had reluctantly returned to Charleston. It had taken Mama herself and all her tact to persuade her to depart.

"Go, Sally," Jenny urged—Jenny who slept in the bed with Ellie most nights when Sally was with Lucy. Ellie was the youngest, the most sensitive, and she'd fastened herself to the aunt who was like her mother. So Sally braced herself to leave her daughters and home.

"Mrs. Thornton, just lift your head a little. There we go!" Open your pretty eyes. That's the way!"

She is forced from her daydream—or was she sleeping? Slowly she opens her eyes.

It's another nurse. Better voice. She doesn't bother to try to identify her. What does she care? She will think of Sally. In her head she often talks to Sally. She tells her about this place, the finest place in the Carolinas. Of course, Thomas would find the best for her. And this—This is the best!

Ah well, 'Old Age is not for Sissies.' She likes that adage. She has it taped to her mirror. Her mirror. The nurse is insisting that she look in this mirror, look at herself. The nurse is adjusting her hair, dusting her face with powder. She pretends to look. She wants the process finished. She wants to return to her own world, to Ashton, to her sisters.

Daphne

❦

Ashton, 1926

ON AN UNSEASONABLY BALMY SUNDAY afternoon in mid-winter, Daphne and Jenny were entertaining their gentlemen callers on the wide front porch. Daphne was in a corner, literally surrounded by swains. Mama was right, it was high time she made a choice among her suitors. Two of her beaus had actually joined forces and confronted her together, insisting that she choose one or another. She stalled and vacillated, bestowing kisses and embraces as necessary to keep them in line.

On this particular Sunday afternoon Daphne was spreading her smiles and compliments evenly among her beaus when she saw Sam Collins break away from her orbit and drift over to the banister where he lit a cigarette. After a few puffs, he tossed it aside and ambled toward Jenny. Why, he was actually elbowing his way in so he could sit on the arm of her chair! Of all things, after he had hung around Daphne for the last five years declaring undying love. She leaned forward to be sure. Yes! That brat Jenny had turned her back on her own beaus and was flirting with Sam. Well, she'd fix her. The day would never come when Jenny, who wasn't even really pretty, could take a man away from *her*.

But just then she heard an automobile pull up into the driveway—probably Mary, being returned from her weekend visit to Camden. Jack Sterling said, "Why, it's a Pierce Arrow. No one around here has one. Who could it belong to?"

Mary emerged and came up to join them, accompanied by a man Daphne had never seen before. His looks were unexceptional, though pleasant— average height, brown hair, nice features. But there was something about his clothes, the cut and the fit, the very material, that set him apart. He looked like a city man. He looked rich.

"Hello, everybody," Mary's face was flushed, her eyes shining. "This is Mr. Kevin Worthington. He's spending the season in Camden."

Mama and Papa appeared and the group drifted into the parlor. It seemed that Mr. Worthington had brought his horses all the way from Louisville, Kentucky, to winter in South Carolina and compete in the steeplechase. He and his trainer were headquartered with friends. He named the Yankee family that had purchased the largest of the old Camden homes.

Daphne took a deep breath—someone different, someone from far away, someone who was surely rich. Very rich. And here he was with *Mary*. Oh, what could she do?

After the men left, Mary turned to Mama, and the words began tumbling out. "Kevin asked me to a dinner dance Wednesday night. I can stay with cousin Lou, again—Mama, we met on Friday and he invited me to lunch and the race, then dinner on Saturday, we had such a good time together—and I've got that beautiful pink material Lyda gave me. If you help, we can make a dress by Wednesday."

"I'll get started in the morning," Mama said.

Mary left on Wednesday, driven by an uncharacteristically subdued Papa, who had made no objection to any of the plans. It was agreed that Mary would invite Mr. Worthington to Sunday supper.

How, oh how was Daphne going to get Mr. Worthington's attention? She entertained not a moment's doubt that she could appropriate him once he noticed her. But how to accomplish this? Mary was easy to deceive but Mama was not.

When Sunday evening arrived, Papa gathered the family to go to All Saints Church for Evensong, a service Mama never missed. Mr. Worthington was expected at eight o'clock, leaving plenty of time for the service and last minute preparations.

"I've got a headache," Daphne said. "I'll stay

home and lie down, then get the table set when I've rested awhile. It'll be so quiet with Dukie and Josephine out of the way. I'll call them inside in plenty of time."

She had neither a headache nor a plan, but she certainly didn't want to sit through a second church service. She noticed that Mary hesitated—*oh surely she wasn't going to stay home, too*. But Mary ended by putting on her hat and trailing along.

The family group had been gone about fifteen minutes when she heard a car drive up. She rushed to the porch. It was the Pierce Arrow!

"Why, Mr. Worthington, please come on up."

He started up the stairway, hat in hand. "I was in the neighborhood looking at a horse I'm thinking of buying. Since we finished so quickly, I thought I might walk around until your family returned from church—I do hope I'm not disturbing you."

Daphne's mind was whirling. This was her chance—but what to do? She began by looking him straight in the eye and bestowing upon him her most dazzling smile.

"Why, not at all," she said.

Ah, yes, his eyes showed that he was noticing her now, all right. In fact, his eyes flickered over her from head to toe and he stepped forward, beaming, to shake hands.

"You're Miss Daphne. I remember from last Sunday."

Turning to lead the way into the parlor, she stubbed her toe on the doorsill.

"Oh," she murmured, swaying. He was beside her in a moment, catching her by the shoulders.

"I—I think I twisted my ankle."

"Don't put any weight on it," he said. "Lean on me." She did so. His arms tightened. She turned to smile at him—a shy smile this time—providing a view of her pretty profile.

He bent his head toward hers, his eyes on her lips.

This was her chance. She would have to risk his thinking her fast. She *would* risk it. She lifted her face and he closed his mouth on hers. She felt his heart begin to pound and kissed him back for just a moment before she drew away.

"Oh, no, Mr. Worthington—"

"Kevin, call me Kevin." His voice was husky. "Please forgive me, Daphne, may I call you Daphne?"

His arms were still around her, but loosely now.

"Let me help you. You mustn't put any weight on that ankle." He scooped her up, placed her on the uncomfortable love seat by the fireplace and sat down close beside her.

"I was carried away—you're just so lovely. Please do forgive me, let me take a look at that ankle."

She lifted her shapely left leg and he closed his hand around her slim ankle. It was terribly improper, and they both knew it.

"No swelling yet." He was still holding her ankle. He sounded breathless. "I'll get you a footstool. It should be elevated."

He sat back down beside her and she turned to smile at him. "Oh, Kevin—"

He stopped her words by pulling her into his arms and kissing her again, more insistently this time. She returned his kiss and let him press her close against his chest before she broke away.

"This is terrible behavior. Kevin, I've never, ever acted this way before. We must stop right now."

"I can't stop what I'm feeling." He grasped her hand and kissed it.

"Mary, we must think of Mary," she murmured.

He straightened, still holding her hand.

"Listen Daphne, there's nothing at all between Mary and me but a friendship. I like her. I like your whole family and all the local people I've met. The horse crowd gets tedious. I like being with the real South Carolinians—when they deign to associate with me. But you, you're—well, I'll just have to admit that I'm bowled over. Please, please give me a chance. Let's try to really get to know one another."

Daphne lowered her eyes.

"You'll have to explain to Mary," she said. "Be sure she understands it's just a friendship. We sisters never interfere with each other's beaus."

"I'll clear things up with her tonight. Then, Daphne, will you come to Camden so I can be with you away from ... from so many people?"

So many Willoughbys, he meant. With Mama and Papa and sisters all over the place, it was a wonder any of them ever managed to fall in love and marry.

"Can't you stay with that same aunt? There are parties this weekend, we could have such fun."

Just then a car drove up. Daphne sprang to her feet, forgetting the twisted ankle. He rose, straightening his tie and jacket. They were standing well apart but still flushed when Mary rushed in, followed by Mama and Papa.

Mama had encountered one of the Thornton brothers at church and asked him to join them for supper. A longtime admirer of Daphne's, Frank hurried over to sit beside her on the love seat. She explained about her twisted ankle and sank down, aware that Kevin had placed himself directly across the room so that he could keep her in his line of vision. She turned and gave her attention to Frank, to his great surprise and delight, but every time she raised her eyes, they met Kevin's.

Jenny helped Mama and the servants in the after-dinner cleanup and Papa retired to his library. She observed with satisfaction that Kevin guided Mary out to the porch, where they seemed to be engaged in earnest conversation. When the men departed, Mary went straight to her room, looking quite stricken.

So he's told her. Daphne felt a pang of shame and sympathy but she stifled the feeling. It was all very well for Mama and Papa and Lucy to be so noble, but she was different. She would *not* feel distress for Mary. She was going to look out for herself.

* * *

When the telephone range at noon on Monday, Daphne answered.

"Daphne? It's Kevin. Will you come to Camden for the weekend? Now, please, don't say no, don't say maybe. Just listen. I can pick you up Friday or whenever you're free. You can stay with my friends, the Smithers, unless your parents insist on that aunt's. We'll have the whole weekend, I'll drive you back as late as you'll let me on Sunday night. *Will* you come?"

"I'll come on the train, that'll be best. It should get to Camden about four o'clock Friday. I'm sure it'll be Aunt Lou's for headquarters."

"That's wonderful, Daphne, just great. I'll ring back later in the week to confirm everything."

It was a hard week for Daphne at Ashton. When she told Mama her plans, the look she received would have squelched almost anyone, but Daphne brazened it out. Mary was cool but composed. Thank heavens Mary, as the oldest, now had a bedroom to herself. Jenny treated her with studied reserve. Worst of all, Papa invited her in to his library and closed the door.

He turned his black eyes on her, looking straight into hers. Her heart began to thump, but no, she was *not* going to cry.

When he spoke, it was in a quiet voice, a voice more sorrowful than angry.

"I try to keep out of these flirtations that occupy you girls, but I feel I must speak up when there appears to be a matter of less than honorable behavior. Now, what is this I hear about your having appropriated Mr. Worthington, who arrived here under the auspices of friendship with Mary?"

In spite of herself, she felt almost sick. What was that hold that Papa had over them all? Why was it so terrible to displease him? Anyway, she'd always felt that she wasn't good enough for Papa and Mama. All her sisters knew she lacked something that the rest of them had and she knew it, too.

She would stand right up to Papa!

"Mr. Worthington and Mary had only a very casual friendship, Papa. He has assured me of this. He's invited me to a nice series of parties. Surely we're allowed to exchange friends with each other? After all, our choices are pretty limited around here."

Papa looked at her, long and steadily. Then he sighed.

"Obviously the damage to Mary's friendship has already been done. We shall not now cry over spilt milk. Go along, Daphne. But let me just caution you. True happiness is never built upon the distress of others."

He turned away and she left the room. It bothered her, all right, but she wasn't going to think about it anymore. This was her chance. She'd never get another one stuck away in the country. What did she care what Papa thought? He seemed to care mighty little about her opinion. She was going to find something decent to wear if she had to sneak into every wardrobe in the house. She was going to Camden and that was that.

* * *

While she gathered clothes together for the weekend, pretending not to notice the cool atmosphere surrounding her, Daphne began to assess her situation regarding Kevin and her future.

The Willoughby girls had been made thoroughly aware not only of the importance of being born to be ladies, but also of always acting like ladies. No lady behaved as she had with Kevin. How was she to recover her position? She was well indoctrinated in the prevailing wisdom that when the time came for marriage, a gentleman chose a lady. A man wanted a woman of unquestioned virtue for the mother of his children.

By Friday, she had decided on her plan of action.

She emerged from the train, carrying her bag, and Kevin, springing forward eagerly to take it from her, bent to kiss her. She stepped back.

"Heavens, Kevin, all these people might be

strangers to you, but lots of them know exactly who I am."

He drew back and took her arm, but as soon as he had her seated in his big automobile, he slid into the driver's side and leaned over her, pressing her against the seat and kissing her urgently.

After a moment, she pulled away and put her face in her hands and began to cry softly.

"Daphne, darling, what's the matter? Is it something I've done?"

"It's not your fault, Kevin—it's mine. I've behaved—not at all like a lady, letting you kiss me when we hardly know each other. I just don't know what came over me, but I know my parents would be horrified. I'm upset with myself—how can you possibly respect me? We shouldn't see each—"

"Daphne!" he pulled her hands from her face and held them gently in his. Fortunately, her eyes were full of tears.

"Please don't talk this way. I do respect you, I understand your background and the way you were raised. It's my fault, I'm carried away with such strong feelings for you, I'm so grateful that you seem to return them in some small way, I'll control myself. We'll start again."

She turned a tremulous, dimpled smile on him and said, "Thank you, Kevin. I'm so relieved you understand."

The weekend's dinners and balls were sprinkled with Baskins, Tulles, Harringtons, all cousins or longtime family friends of the Willoughbys. The winter people—Northerners—gathered around Daphne, appearing to find her company delightful. Kevin conducted himself impeccably. He was obviously proud and was certainly attentive to the point of possessiveness, but he took no further liberties. They were seldom alone for more than a few moments.

He drove her home at dusk Sunday. She insisted they arrive at Ashton before dark. Just before they reached the road that led to her house, he pulled the car onto a sheltered spot and parked. Then he turned and took her hands.

"Daphne, I'm falling in love with you. I promised to behave properly and I will. I'll pursue a very correct courtship until I make you love me a little in return, but, please, just one kiss?"

She turned her face to his and he grasped her tightly before she had a chance to say a word.

At length, she pulled away. She knew what it was he loved about her better than he did, and she also knew that she would have to use it if she were going to get the proposal she had set her heart on.

In the remaining weeks before the final Camden steeplechase, Kevin and Daphne were together every weekend. When he appeared at Ashton for midweek calls, Mama treated him with courtesy, as did the other girls. They were well aware that he was the innocent party in the whole episode. Mary, meantime, spent most evenings in the company of faithful Ned.

The steeplechase weekend was an unqualified success. One of Kevin's horses came in second and the celebration that followed at the Smithers' home lasted most of the night. Daphne had never been to such a sophisticated party. Champagne flowed. Toasts were followed not only by smashed glasses but also by indiscriminate embracing and kissing. Kevin missed no chance to grab her for a kiss when that part of the ceremony began. Some of the men and women struck Daphne as very rough types, hardly ladies and gentlemen at all. They used words she had never heard spoken before, and she was only vaguely aware of their improper meanings. But she had no intention of acting like a country innocent. She laughed, took tiny sips of her champagne and furtively encouraged the considerable male attention she was attracting. She could tell that Kevin was jealous. By the end of the evening, he never left her side and it was he who suggested that it was time for her to go to Aunt Lou's. Poor old Aunt Lou, Mama must not realize how senile she had become or she would never have allowed Daphne to stay there.

Before Kevin left for Louisville, he extracted her promise and Mama's agreement that she would visit his home very soon.

* * *

Some weeks later Daphne was on the train heading for Kentucky. Both Mama and Daphne had received gracious letters on heavy, cream paper inviting her for this visit. Mama seemed to have accepted the inevitable. She helped Daphne make a new dress and remodel several others. All skirts were shortened to the limit of what Mama would permit.

The family was, as usual, absorbed in the older girls. Lucy was occupied with her adored baby boy. Sally, whose life struck Daphne as horrible as a pulp magazine serial, was now embroiled in trouble because Crawford was involved in some disgraceful mess. Their little girls were ensconced at Ashton being petted and spoiled.

Mary had married Ned in a quiet family ceremony. Daphne was glad to leave it all behind.

Kevin met her, beaming and eager. "One kiss, oh, please," he said when they were settled in the Pierce Arrow. He didn't wait for her answer but folded her in his arms and kissed her until she finally pulled away, breathless.

"No more, now Kevin. You must promise not to tempt me or yourself. Mama would die if I behaved other than as a perfect lady when I'm in another person's home and another *state*, even."

As they drove through the lovely, hilly city, she was charmed with everything she saw. Then, when well outside the city on acres of rolling green, they drew up in front of the Worthington home, Daphne could hardly contain her excitement. The house was a large Georgian structure of mellow old brick. Formal gardens surrounded it. Rich! Certainly these people were rich, just as rich and grand as she had dreamed.

A white-coated Negro met them at the door. Another servant materialized to take her bags from the car. Then Mrs. Worthington appeared in the vast formal hallway. Could this lovely, stylish, young-looking woman really be the mother of grown men?

"My dear, at last." She extended both hands to Daphne and kissed her on the cheek. "Why, Kevin, she's just as lovely as you said. I didn't believe him for a minute, he's far too infatuated to judge, but here you are, beautiful and from the Deep South, as well. I'm from Mobile, Alabama, myself, and these Kentuckians are not real southerners. You and I must team up and show them what it means to be a true southerner."

Her accent was still Alabama, even if her appearance bespoke New York, at least for shopping trips.

Daphne was delighted. The Willoughby and Abbott charm and confidence came automatically. She dimpled up at her delightful hostess and joined in the pleasantries. When Mr. Worthington came in, although elegantly dressed, he seemed quite old enough to be the father of grown sons. He was gracious but taciturn, leaving his wife in charge.

At eight o'clock, Daphne came down for dinner, having changed into her second best dress, a pale blue silk with a dropped waist and a brief skirt.

Kevin's brother and sister-in-law with their two small sons had gathered in the large, elegantly appointed front room.

The brother, Josh, was quite like his father. Kevin had explained that as the older son, although only by one year, he helped his father in the large machinery business that seemed to be the foundation of the family fortune. Kevin, who loved and understood horse flesh, had the job of running the Worthington stables. He bought, bred, and trained race horses. This enterprise was supposed to turn a profit and generally did.

"Being from South Carolina, I'm pretty familiar with horses," Daphne managed to turn the full wattage of her smile on both Josh and his father. "But I don't know much about machinery. Just what sort of things do you make at the Worthington Works?"

The ensuing explanation occupied most of the cocktail hour.

But when Daphne tried her charm on Christina, the daughter-in-law, she met with considerably less success. This large young woman was dressed as if for a morning with her sons. She wore a tweed skirt, not nearly short enough, and a plain white blouse. The only interest she showed was in the horses when she was able to get a few words with Kevin. Apparently she was an avid horsewoman; an excellent rider, her boys as well, Kevin explained. When the mint juleps had been consumed, the boys were led away by a uniformed maid, and the group proceeded into the elegant dining room where three white-coated men served with quiet efficiency.

It was a perfect week. Friends gave small dinners in her honor. She and Mrs. Worthington called on two aged aunts one afternoon at tea time. Kevin showed her around the extensive stables and took her for a brief visit to the machine works. One evening they ate a light supper with Josh and Christina who Daphne thought was a cold fish and terribly plain looking, as well. She observed with satisfaction that Christina and her mother-in-law seemed on rather distant formal terms; whereas she herself found Mrs. Worthington quite the nicest and most congenial person she had met in Louisville.

They chatted easily and happily at every opportunity. Mrs. Worthington admitted to a special soft spot for her younger son, and was quite open in her approval of Daphne.

On the last evening of the visit, the Worthingtons went to a dinner party, leaving the young couple to be fed and chaperoned by the servants. Kevin invited Daphne for a stroll in the gardens. She was about to have offered to her what she had sought for so long.

"I love you and want you for my wife, Daphne. Please say you'll marry me." He pulled a diamond ring from his pocket and slipped it on her finger. It glittered in the moonlight, larger and brighter than any diamond she had ever seen.

"Will you, Daphne? Will you marry me?"

"Oh, yes," she breathed.

Then she was crushed in his arms and he was kissing her with such vigor that she lost her breath. She was becoming quite uncomfortable in his strong grasp and struggled a bit to push away.

"No, no," he said against her lips. "At last, at last you're mine," and he held her hard in his arms until they heard his parents' car in the driveway.

Sally

Atlanta 1926

Cousin Edwin met Sally at the Atlanta train station in a long black Buick automobile. He was tall, white-haired, distinguished-looking.

"You must be Sally." He removed his hat. "A strong family resemblance."

Sally's spirits rose. She and cousin Edwin talked easily as they rolled down Peachtree Road, Sally praising every sight and sound. Cousin Edwin beamed with pride in his great city. He introduced her to Mrs. Brown and left after arranging that his driver would collect Sally for dinner.

His house was a vast Tudor structure in Ansley Park, his wife stylish and good-looking. She offered a cigarette, Sally accepted; a cocktail, Sally declined. But that didn't stop cousin Roberta and cousin Edwin. The black butler-driver, now white-coated for his butler duties, brought them dry martinis on a silver tray. Sally was entranced.

One purpose of the Atlanta plan was that Sally would see Crawford the first Sunday of each month, which was all that was permitted. But this dreaded duty was three weeks away. Sally put it to the back of her mind and entered her new life with zest. She kept her longing for her daughters at bay but she wrote a brief note to each of them every day that she spent in Atlanta.

Cousin Edwin's array of offices was located on Peachtree Road, like most things in Atlanta. It was right in the heart of the bustling city.

Sally had ridden the trolley, arriving early and excited. A matronly black clad woman escorted her to the "typist pool." The girls were friendly, she heard southern accents everywhere. Sally's Abbott-Willoughby confidence had taken a bad blow in the last months but it was still there, lying in wait. She was easy, warm, natural, her old self, or almost.

She fell upon her work with a vengeance. The days flew by. Then it was time to take the trolley to the federal prison. She steeled herself.

My God, could that be Crawford the guard was leading in? Oh Crawford, Crawford! He had a pallor like none she'd ever seen before. His yellowed fingers trembled as he lit a cigarette. But then he smiled— Yes, Crawford!

"Hello darling Sally," he murmured through the bars that separated them. "You are indeed a sight for these sore old eyes—"

"You're not half bad yourself. In fact, you look

very well indeed. The regime here must agree with you."

"Well, the liquids served are good for my digestion and my figure. Wish I'd thought of an easier route to sobriety."

"Me too," she said.

Then they both laughed.

She began to tell him about the girls.

"They sound so smart, like their mother."

"They're good-looking—like their father."

They managed. He thanked her for coming. "I love you Sally, I always will," he said at the end.

It was over.

* * *

She'd worked for a month when Mr. Colvin Withers stopped at her desk, introduced himself, and asked her to step into his office. She'd noticed him. He was youngish, nice-looking in a sturdy, clean cut, blond sort of way. He had a southern accent, probably Atlanta. There were quite a few Yankees on the sales staff but none as highly placed as Mr. Withers appeared to be. His large corner office was elegantly appointed. He introduced her to Mrs. Reeves, his secretary, who had a room of her own guarding his.

"Please sit down, Mrs. Carsworth." The chair was soft, real leather. "I hear great things about you. Mrs. Reeves is leaving the city, rather suddenly—

next week, in fact. Would you like to try her job?" The salary he named took her breath away. "The work will be harder. You'll have to stay late some evenings. Will that be a problem?"

"No, Mr. Withers, I'd like very much to try it."

She treated herself to a long-distance call to Ashton that night. She talked to both girls, told Papa the news and then heard, "Your three minutes are up." Surely it had only been three seconds?

The next day she went into Rich's department store, the most magnificent shopping emporium she had ever seen or imagined. She didn't just look, which she'd done before, but purchased—a new blouse, a black skirt, short, very short. Papa would never see it, but she was proud of her legs and all the other girls wore just such skirts.

She arrived early for her first day with Mr. Withers but he was there ahead of her. He was cordial—gracious even—but went straight to work at a fast pace. It took all of her skill to keep up with his rapid dictation, all of her speed to get the typing done.

The days flew by. Then one day at five o'clock he stepped out to her desk. She liked the way he did that, instead of ringing a bell for her to come into his office like most of the other bosses did.

He's a gentleman, she thought. That helps.

"Mrs. Carsworth, would you be able to stay late tonight, perhaps two hours?"

"Certainly, Mr. Withers."

It seemed he was closing an important sale. She became quite interested in the letters she was taking down and typing for his signature.

"Well, that finishes it." He looked at his watch. "I didn't realize. It's eight o'clock. I'll drive you home."

"Oh, no. The streets are well lighted—I'll be fine."

"I insist. You're right on my way."

His face was so open and that appealing smile. He was waiting for her to answer, watching her intently.

But how did he know where she lived? Well, it seemed ungracious to refuse and besides she was tired. His sporty-looking car was the only one left in the parking lot. He opened the door for her.

"I live only a block away from Mr. Abbott. He and Miss Roberta are both so awfully nice. I understand he's a cousin of yours."

"Yes." She felt her face flush. *Dear Lord, does he know everything about me?*

"You're doing such good work, Mrs. Carsworth. If the load's too heavy, just say so—we can always draw on the typing pool for extra help. You can recommend whom we should call." He smiled at her. Sally smiled back. She'd heard some of the women be patronized, or spoken to sharply. She'd hate that. Was he treating her as if she were a partner, like himself, because she was kin to the boss? No, it was probably because he was a gentleman.

He seemed quite secure in his position. He appeared to be second in command to cousin Edwin, who happened to be childless. She'd have to nose around a little bit during her lunch break with the typing girls.

He walked her to Mrs. Brown's door, removed his hat to say goodnight, took the key and opened the door for her when she had a little struggle with the lock. He was a gentleman. She was lucky.

Her hints the next day at lunch brought forth full details. Mr. Withers was thirty-six years old but still not married. His photograph or name sometimes appeared on the society page of *The Atlanta Constitution*. He was known to be a member of the Piedmont Driving Club and the Nine O'clocks. He still occasionally squired debutantes around. He had once been engaged—Belle, the best informed of his admirers, was sure of this information. The girl had broken it off at the last moment and married someone else instead.

"He was just devastated, it's why he's still single," Belle said. It was also why he worked so hard—which was, in turn, the cause of his rapid rise in the company. The bookkeeper, who was fortunately in attendance at this particular lunch, was able to supply his exact income for the previous year. Sally felt almost faint when she heard the magnificent sum. Belle, the avid newspaper reader, was possessed of the information that his family was a wealthy one. They owned important real estate.

That's why he had gone into the business. Sally would have been quite cowed when she returned to her desk at two p.m. had she not been an Abbott and a Willoughby. After all, where were an Atlantan's ancestors likely to have been when hers were signing the Declaration of Independence?

The late nights at work occurred rather frequently, and Sally now accepted the ride home without protest. She enjoyed chatting with him. He asked about her home, seemed interested in the old plantation and her many sisters. He never asked about her present life, so she knew he knew. He was, after all, very close to cousin Edwin. He had been at the University of Virginia with several Charleston men. She knew them all well, told him news of them. He now drove very slowly when he took her home. Was he taking a circuitous route? Sally knew she must be very careful. He liked her too much. She couldn't help liking him in return—too much?

She didn't like his knowing about her situation, but he gave no slightest hint of this knowledge. He was indeed a gentleman. Although his courtesy never failed, he worked very hard.

After two months, she approached his desk.

"Mr. Withers, since your work load seems a little less urgent just now, I wondered if it would be convenient for me to have next Friday and next Monday off? I'd like to go to South Carolina to see my family."

He got to his feet. "Certainly. Absolutely. It's a very good time, feel free to ask any time you need to be away. We can always arrange something from the pool."

Oh, my girls, my girls ... She would see them.

When she did, Atlanta vanished from her mind as if it had been a dream. This was her real life.

Papa, Mama and Lucy met her at the train station with Liz and Ellie. The girls flung themselves at her, their dark eyes shining, their thin little arms clutching her legs. She scooped them both up and kissed every surface she could reach.

As soon as they arrived at Ashton, Liz raced to her room. "I'm in a third grade reader now!" she shouted over her shoulder. "I can read it all, I'll show you."

"I can read it too," Ellie said, climbing on her lap and snuggling as close as she could get. "Aunt Mary lets me read with Liz's class 'cause I can keep right up!"

"Oh, my smart daughters. Show me everything you've learned."

It was a wrench to leave them but she was reassured that they seemed so well and happy. Oh what would she do without her family? Her family was her greatest blessing on this earth. But Papa had not looked well. They said he'd been sick, nothing serious but she was worried.

When she got to the office Tuesday morning, Mr. Withers rose from his desk, beaming.

"So nice to have you back. I hope you found your family well and enjoyed your visit. We missed you."

The days flew by. She grew accustomed to the visits with Crawford, no longer dreaded them but rather enjoyed their talks. At least he was, finally, entirely sober.

Sometimes she ate dinner with her co-workers at one of the downtown restaurants. When the bright city lights came on, she felt as if she were in New York. The Abbotts had her over regularly. She made herself very lively, good company, there being no other way to repay their kindness. They offered to introduce her to some Atlanta women her age—she knew they meant her class—but she declined. "It's best to keep my life simple." They understood.

One evening she accompanied them to the Driving Club. She dressed carefully in her one good party frock, a bright red crepe—sleeveless with a dropped waist, a scooped out neckline, and a short skirt, very short, just grazing her kneecaps. She thought of Mrs. Carsworth when she completed her outfit by adding the pearls her mother-in-law had given her. Funny how seldom she thought of her and poor Eloise.

Well, she gave me one useful thing anyway.

The pearls were very fine ones.

Later at the club, when Sally and the Abbotts had been ceremoniously guided and settled at a small table that bristled with white starched linen and shown with candles and crystal, she looked around the room and found her eyes gazing straight into those of Mr. Withers.

His face lit up and he all but sprinted across the beautiful dining room floor to speak to her.

To speak? I think he's going to spend the evening with us.

"Will you sit down, Colvin?" Cousin Edwin asked. He summoned the waiter with a slight inclination of his head. "Do join Roberta and me in a martini. We can't tempt Sally on that score."

"Thank you, I will." They talked, he lingered. Finally cousin Roberta said gently, "I think your table is waiting dinner for you, Colvin."

"Good heavens. Excuse me for delaying yours." His face flushed and he rushed away.

Oh, she knew all right, and now the boss and his wife knew, too. He was falling for her. She liked him, she liked him all too much. What could she do? This could ruin everything.

She was supporting herself, sending money home to help with her girls and even saving a little bit. She couldn't afford trouble. But she liked his liking her, she couldn't help it. Her life had been so dreary, so desperate, for such a long time. She liked men. No, she loved men. They loved her in return. She refused to worry. They would continue as usual. She would hold the line firmly.

But Mr. Withers was beginning to keep her late

almost every night. If it was only thirty minutes past the closing hour, he would insist on driving her home. He certainly behaved properly. Very businesslike in the office, friendly, but no more on their drives home.

One night when it was really late, almost nine o'clock, he apologized vigorously for the imposition and pulled up in front of an elegant-looking restaurant.

"Oh no," she said, "I really must go straight home."

"Please, Mrs. Carsworth, I'm starving and you must surely be hungry, too. It's perfectly proper, I assure you. Co-workers eat meals together after and during work hours all the time. This is a very nice family restaurant. Please, Mrs. Carsworth."

They went in. If this was a family restaurant, she had certainly not yet seen an expensive, cosmopolitan one. Oh, well, she was here and she proposed to enjoy herself. Stylishly dressed couples were drinking cocktails as if they had never heard of Prohibition. Well, they did that in Charleston, too. She was twenty-eight years old, twice a mother, surely she could cope with one nice man. Several people spoke to him. He paused and introduced her, with no mention of her status as his secretary. In fact, he referred to her as Sally Carsworth. The headwaiter, who knew him, ushered them to a quiet corner. She refused a cocktail but joined him in a cigarette. She was having a good time. She looked around eagerly. She laughed and sparkled. She would sparkle up to her death. It was her essence.

His eyes scarcely left her face. How in the world was he eating while staring at her? She attacked her own plate with gusto. French food!

"Mrs. Carsworth, would it be all right—I mean, it seems so unnatural—would it offend you if I called you Sally? Just out of the office, of course, and would you please oblige me by calling me Colvin? I mean when we're not in the office?"

"Mr. Withers," she said, fastening her shiny black eyes on him, "we should never have occasion to call each other anything except in the office."

"Oh, please don't be offended. I like you so much, hold you in such high esteem, I would never willingly offend you. Your work is perfect, so nice to work with someone like oneself."

He was becoming hopelessly entangled.

She laughed. Then he laughed, too, and the tension eased.

"Is it all right, then?"

"Yes." Nothing that happened to her would transform Sally Willoughby into a prude. She relaxed and had a good time, the best time she'd had in years. Mr. Withers told her about the Atlanta of his childhood, moved on to a few tales of his years at the University of Virginia with the Charleston boys. "That Charleston crowd can lead one astray in the blink of an eye," he said. "Glad you didn't spend your whole lifetime there." His stories made her laugh. His ardent gaze made her blush.

Still, it was almost midnight before she insisted that they leave. No improper word had been spoken. But they both knew. He was falling for her, and now he could no longer hide it. She liked him in return, but she refused to think about it. It was impossible—impossible. Could he hide his feelings in the office? He tried hard. She resisted further dinner invitations. But in the car, he called her Sally. He turned to look at her so often she was afraid he might drive off the road.

Then it was time to go home for Daphne's wedding. She had saved the money, bought a dress, sent money for clothes for her girls. Mr. Withers—in the car she avoided calling him anything—insisted on driving her to the train station. As she was leaving straight from work, it was awkward to refuse.

"We should leave now, don't you think?" he said.

Well, yes, if we want to sit for an hour in the station. But she smiled and rose—secretary-like, she hoped. They did have an hour to wait. He took her to a nearby restaurant, she supposed it was actually a bar. She had refused to go to the Capital City Club when he suggested that. In the bar, which was handsome and quite suitable for ladies—there were many there—he persuaded her to have a glass of wine.

"Sally," he began, "I know about your husband and daughters. Mr. Edwin confided in me before you came. I can't tell you how sorry I am that you have had such trouble. So unfair. I admire you more—much more—than I know how to say. Can't we please be friends? You could talk to me, tell me about your daughters, let me help you maybe in some small way?"

"Colvin," she said his name for the first time, "you are one of the kindest persons I've ever met. You already help me quite enough. I love my job. You are considerate and easy to work for in every way. I'm already most grateful."

"Just think about it while you are gone—a friend-ship, entirely outside the office, of course. You might go with me to dinner without worrying so, to a movie, or a play. Just proper things."

"Colvin," she said it again, "I'm married. It's never proper for a married woman to go around anywhere with a man not her husband."

He looked stricken.

"Don't worry about your job, Sally, never for a moment. Nothing affects that. You are great at your job. Anyone would place high value on your work. I would rather die than cause you worry or distress. I only want what you can spare me of your com-pany. I want to add a little pleasure to your life, if possible. Where's the harm?"

"I'll think about it. We'd better go now."

* * *

Back at Ashton, Sally would scarcely let her girls out of her sight. Oh, how could she bring herself to leave them again? The specter of the next separation hung over the visit like a cloud. Liz and Ellie clung to their mother, knowing she would leave soon.

Papa looked alarmingly frail, Mama looked tired. And small wonder. They had done their very best to fulfill Daphne's desire for a wedding that would impress the Louisville Worthingtons. Of course they were exhausted.

Lucy and Tom drove Sally to the train that was to take her back to Atlanta. The sisters both cried at the parting. Well, it was better than crying in front of her girls.

"You look after them, too, Lucy," Sally said. "They can't have too much love and attention with their mother gone."

"Please don't worry about Liz and Ellie. They are surrounded by love. Take care of yourself, darling Sally."

And so the brief visit ended.

Mr. Withers' face lit up and he sprang to his feet when Sally came in the following Monday. But he controlled himself admirably and she dived into the work that had piled up.

At the end of the week it all ended. The phone at her desk rang.

"Mr. Withers' office," she said, as usual.

"Sally, it's me, Jenny. Papa's had a heart attack. We think he's going to live but he's pretty sick. You'd better come."

She flew in to Mr. Withers' office. He called cousin Edwin, who then summoned cousin Roberta, who helped Sally pack. She took everything. She knew she wouldn't be back.

The next day when the doorbell rang well ahead of train time, it was not cousin Edwin but Mr. Withers who stood before Sally. Hat in hand, he explained that he had come to drive her to the station. He was a full hour earlier that necessary but she was ready. After hugs and kisses all around, Sally finished her goodbyes and they set off.

Sally began, "You ... you'd just better leave me, Mr. Withers."

"Colvin, Sally—Colvin."

"Yes, well, Colvin, we're so early. I have a book to read while I wait. You'll be needed back at the office."

"No, I have something to say ... Please indulge me. Hear me out."

He pulled into a parking space, well away from any other cars. Then he rolled the windows down, admitting a soft breeze, and turned to face her.

"Sally, I'll try not to embarrass you with a display of emotion. But I have to tell you how much you mean to me."

His face was earnest, his feelings clear, Sally felt her eyes filling. She'd had too much trouble and sorrow. This blatant admiration touched a well-spring.

"Don't say anymore, Colvin." Her tears spilled over.

"Sally." His arms came around her. He pulled out a big linen handkerchief and mopped her face. She lifted her head and quickly, before she could move, he bent down and kissed her hard.

For just a moment she yielded. Then she drew back fast and sat against the door.

"No, Colvin, no. I've acted all kinds of a fool in my life but I'll never cheat. I'll never go back on my vow ... for better, for worse."

It took him a few beats, but he rose to the occasion. "Certainly, Sally. I understand. But if it ends, your marriage, I mean, or if there is anything I can do for you ever, will you let me know?"

"Thank you, Colvin. I'll never forget you."

So the Atlanta venture ended and Sally headed home.

The sun is warming her sore old bones but it is gentled by the leaves of the sheltering tree. She hears voices. It is afternoon?

She thinks of Mama—her lovely, sweet mother. She was suppose to be the sweetest sister, the most like Mama. She's glad Mama doesn't know how unsweet she has become. She looks around her. Yes, the faces are mostly dour, dreary. Hard to be sweet for nine decades, too tiring, too much trouble. She pretends to sleep, enjoys deceiving the overbearing nurses.

The voices fade. Is she dreaming? She is no longer in the here and now.

Daphne

Ashton 1926

DAPHNE SINGLE-MINDEDLY PURSUED HER plans for a wedding that would impress her future in-laws, leaving the others to worry about Sally's problems or any other matter that might interfere with what she wanted. Ned and Mary had moved into Ashton so that Ned could take over the farm, which Papa was now too frail to handle. Jenny occupied herself with Sally's girls and her own stable of beaus, but Mary could be pressed into service, and Daphne didn't hesitate to do so.

Mama and Papa, aging and preoccupied with Sally's daughters, agreed to her plans and did their very best to fulfill Daphne's desire for a wedding that would impress the Louisville Worthingtons. The old church glowed in candlelight. Ashton, too, was lit by candles and there were flowers everywhere. A string quartet played in the parlor. Papa had permitted champagne!

Daphne's in-laws had no trouble recognizing the quality of their new relatives.

And so she became Mrs. Kevin Worthington and proceeded north with her bridegroom to board the great ocean liner for Europe. She was rich and far away, at last. Now she would be happy.

* * *

Sometimes she could scarcely believe it was she, Daphne Willoughby, who was living through these golden days. Europe! But, strangely, when she stood before the Tower of London or the ancient walls of Windsor Castle, or when she walked through the magnificent mirrored halls of Versailles or among the ruins of ancient Rome, all she could think of was *Papa*.

Papa should be here in her place, Papa, who knew every detail of British history; Papa, who could read French and Latin and even Greek, Papa who had hardly been anywhere—to fight in Virginia when he was sixteen years old, to visit Washington, D.C., when some matter concerning his beloved state justified the expense, around the southern states where cousins lived. Yet Papa knew everything about Europe and here *she* stood, the sister who had refused to listen, who had daydreamed while Papa explained the Norman Conquest, expounded on Louis the Sun King, read to them from *Julius Caesar*, translating as he went. Oh, Papa!

She wrote frequent letters home, addressed to both Mama and Papa, but it was to Papa that she wanted to tell it all. News from home was received infrequently because they moved about so often.

As for Kevin, he'd been to Europe several times and didn't seem very interested.

"Let's go buy you something," he would say.

So she had cardigans from London, dresses from Paris, shoes from Italy. Mostly Kevin was eager to get her back to the various hotel rooms.

One afternoon when he had urged her back to their luxurious suite in early afternoon, she tossed her golden curls and said, "Honestly, Kevin, I think you would have liked it better if we'd spent our honeymoon in a hotel room in Columbia, South Carolina."

He seemed not at all offended. He just laughed and strode across the room to grab her in his arms saying, "You're right. I would have liked it excellently."

When they reached the shores of New York and proceeded to Saratoga to spend a few days so Kevin could check on his horses, Daphne was forced to recognize that what she had thought might be seasickness was something else entirely.

"Oh, Kevin, it's too soon," she said, sobbing in his arms. She knew he thought so too, but apparently the feeling was mitigated by pride in impending fatherhood.

Kevin, hoping to cheer her, urged her to telephone Ashton.

"Listening to your father will cheer you up," he said.

So it was by long distance that she learned that Papa had had a heart attack.

"Oh, Mama, why didn't you let me know?"

"Daphne, dear, he did so well, recovering within days. We didn't want to cast a cloud over your honeymoon when Papa was obviously going to be fine."

She asked to speak to Papa, who was reassuring. "I'm very well, Daphne. Your letters to us were excellent. I've kept them all."

She felt a glow of pride. It was so very nice to have finally pleased Papa. Mama insisted that they go to Louisville and settle in before she even considered a visit to Ashton.

"Mary and Ned are here," she said. "Don't worry about us for a moment."

And to Louisville they went, to the caretaker's cottage on the edge of the Worthington homesite. It had been extensively remodeled and charmingly furnished for their use.

After a few days, Mrs. Worthington called to see if Daphne felt rested enough for her to drop in for a cup of afternoon tea.

"Oh, yes, please come." Daphne's maid and cook, well-trained by her mother-in-law, left her with very little to do besides write thank-you notes and feel ill.

"Daphne," Mrs. Worthington said when they were seated in the living room bay window, "I don't want you to call me 'Mrs.' anymore. I feel too close to you. You already have the most perfect of mothers, so that name is thoroughly taken. How about just 'Anna,' then I could feel like a sister or a friend?"

"Oh, I would love that. Thank you, Anna."

Daphne then proceeded to tell her about the morning sickness. She began to feel that she could tell her almost anything, this lovely, young-seeming person who appeared to have nothing of more importance in her life than Daphne herself. Daphne, the fifth child, the frivolous child, the selfish child, was now the center of a parent's undivided attention.

She began to feel better. Anna saw that she met the right young women, was included in the proper clubs and entertainments. Without Sally and Lucy around, Daphne felt quite intelligent and competent. She was popular and readily accepted in Kevin's circle of friends. Still, always underneath her happiness over this wholehearted acceptance, there was a voice inside her head that just seemed to be saying, "Papa, Mama, Ashton." She missed them. She devoured the letters from home and from her sisters. Lucy, dear Lucy—who could *not* love her?—wrote her regularly with news of all the sisters.

When she heard that Jenny was engaged to Arthur Harrington, she felt a pang—the old feeling she had felt so often at Ashton when one of the sisters had a stroke of good fortune.

Well, she should know by now that Jenny was born under a lucky star. Mama and Papa, old and tired, had permitted Lyda, even Lucy, to be Jenny's surrogate mothers. Jenny was petted, spoiled, *lucky*. Now she had landed the best catch in South Carolina.

Arthur was such a gentleman, his family so distinguished—indeed famous, by local standards. Also, by local standards, he was far from poor. Jenny would have a good life. The sisters and Mama wrote that he adored their Jenny. Jenny would stay right there in South Carolina to be loved and petted by her family, as usual. Why had she ever thought she wanted to be far from her home and family? But she had and she had achieved what she wanted. Why did she not feel content? Why was she not happy?

*

* * *

As the time for the birth of her child drew nearer, Daphne's longing for home and family grew stronger.

There was no question of Mama coming to be with her. She could not leave Papa. Mary was a school teacher and couldn't leave her classroom. So, it was established that Jenny would come.

Daphne sent a train ticket and Kevin met her at

the station with Daphne waiting in the Pierce Arrow, too eager for the reunion to remain at home. The sisters fell into each other's arms, laughing and crying alternately. Oh, Daphne was so very glad to have her sister near—her own flesh and blood. How she had missed *her* people, *her* home, *her* state.

But within a few days the patterns of a lifetime began to emerge. Jenny was an immediate hit, not only with the Worthington family but also with Daphne and Kevin's friends. She was witty, confident, always in motion. Daphne began to feel dull, slow, faded beside all that brunette vibrancy.

Daphne was pleased with Jenny's praise of her home, her clothes, furniture, indeed all of her possessions. Why, she even had her own automobile, an unheard of luxury! But what was so galling was that Jenny didn't seem in the least desirous of such things for herself. She glowed at the mention of her Arthur's name; showed with pride the little old-fashioned cluster of diamonds he had given her, talked eagerly of her wedding plans. She wasn't really impressed with any of the Worthington grandeur. Anyone could see that.

Jenny was just like Mama and Papa. *They're all alike*. Their large spiritedness made her feel small, so small.

At last the day arrived when it was obvious that the birth was imminent. Kevin drove Daphne to the hospital where a specialist was to officiate at the delivery. Jenny waited with Mrs. Worthington and

Kevin through a long afternoon and evening. At almost midnight the doctor emerged beaming—a girl, a beautiful seven-pound baby girl.

Long distance calls were made to Ashton. Kevin dispensed pink-ribboned cigars to everyone in sight. The infant was indeed beautiful.

"Anna," Daphne whispered to her mother-in-law. "She's to be named Anna."

So Jenny went home leaving Daphne surrounded by flowers, trained nurses and lesser servants.

"Daphne, you and Annie will be ready to come to my wedding. It's perfect timing. But we'll keep Annie hidden until we leave for our wedding trip. I'll not be outshone on my own wedding day."

* * *

Kevin, Daphne, Annie and her nurse were indeed ensconced at Ashton by Jenny's wedding day, just as the sisters had planned. Daphne felt such joy at being with Mama and Papa and her sisters that those buried feelings she hated surfaced hardly at all.

I must talk to Mary, Daphne told herself. We should clear the air of any bad feelings about Kevin. But Mary seemed so happy. She and Ned appeared to gravitate toward each other. He often touched her, just her elbow or hand or cheek. His adoration was obvious and Mary had blossomed under its glow.

Thus Daphne left for Louisville reluctantly, with a feeling of unfinished business left behind.

But in just one month she was back at Ashton, shaken to her core by Papa's death. Life without Papa—it could hardly be imagined. Nor could she imagine then how they would never experience life without Papa. He was in their hearts and heads. His words, beliefs, principles would remain with them to the end, not always acted upon or even consciously recognized. But they were never to be free of Papa's benevolent, high-minded dominance.

The sisters comforted each other and clustered protectively around Mama.

"Come on, men," Lyda's husband, as the senior son-in-law, assumed leadership.

"Let's go outside and get out of the ladies' way. Come on, youngsters, leave your Mamas with their Mama and the babies with the nurses. It's nice outside."

The sons-in-law gathered under the old oak tree that had been Lucy's favorite reading hideout. Cigarettes were lit. At least one gentleman usually had a flask to pass around. A strong bond had developed among the men. They shared the same triumph—the winning of a Willoughby belle—and the same nagging discomfort. They just weren't Papa. What a burden to have to follow in the footsteps of the Colonel.

When Papa's triumphant funeral services had concluded, Daphne stayed on with Annie after

Kevin departed. Mama seemed comforted by Annie's presence and spent long hours just holding her or watching her in her carriage.

Daphne and Mary were in the parlor alone one late afternoon when Daphne thought the time had come to bring up the unmentioned breach between them.

"Mary, I want you to know I realize that I behaved badly toward you in regard to Kevin. I do hate having hurt you."

Mary turned an open, shining face toward her.

"Oh, Daphne, that business with Kevin was the best thing that ever happened to me. You know what a hard time I've always had making up my mind about anything. Something had to push me into realizing what a treasure I had in Ned and how close I had come to losing him.

"There's no way for me to tell you how happy we are together. I don't deserve him but I do so much appreciate him and love him. I'd like to have a child," Mary's face became still, "but since it hasn't happened, Ned says it's for the best. He wants my love all to himself."

Mary blushed. "At least, that's what he says. You know, Daphne, I never wanted to get away like you and Sally. I love being at Ashton. I've had Mama and Papa almost to myself. Now I can really be needed by Mama. I love teaching school and I love the children I teach, well, most of them. I never dreamed I could be so happy, and in a way I owe it to you."

Daphne sat stunned. She should have observed Mary's obvious contentment, she should be relieved. She was not, though, she was jealous. Yes, she might as well admit it to herself. She was jealous of such wholehearted happiness. She pulled herself together.

"I'm so glad, Mary, and so relieved."

Daphne no longer even considered such remarks as lies or even fibs. She would never understand a woman like Mary. How could they be sisters?

So when, on the next day, she left Ashton for Louisville, it was with the same old feeling. She was not good enough. She had missed out on blessings her siblings enjoyed.

She was not happy, she was not even content.

Lucy

By the time Thomas entered Ellerton Grammar School, Lucy had put aside her longing for another baby. She buried the disappointment deep inside where the other graver sorrows lay and emersed herself in Thomas' active life.

From the first he was bright and strong. He seemed to excel so effortlessly. Through his early schooling and into high school, he was Lucy's source of greatest satisfaction.

How she and Tom had loved those Friday night high school football games, with everybody they knew out cheering for Ellerton High and Thomas running like the wind, a football tucked under his arm while the crowd rose up and shouted his name. Those were the times when her heart beat fast again and once more a flush of joy would suffuse her face.

Her secret joy was the way Thomas turned to her—for solace, and comfort, of course, she was his mother—but also to share his triumphs. These were the memories she valued most.

"Mother!" he said. He was standing at the front door, books piled under one arm, a football helmet under another, face streaked with dirt. "Guess what?"

"Thomas, I could never guess. Just tell me."

"I've been elected president of the senior class." He was breathing hard. He must have run all the way home so she would be the first to know.

"Oh, Thomas," she folded her arms around him and drew his hard, perspiration-soaked body close. *What did her little frustrations amount to? This is what counts—Thomas. He must be happy. He must be fulfilled.*

When he led the class in on graduation night, a golden ribbon across his chest, his head turned to catch her eye.

Then she was happy. Yes, there had been some very happy times.

Thomas liked to read and think and talk just as she did. They sat by the hour in the old swing that was still on the porch, talking over news and political happenings or, best of all, what he was learning in his history and literature courses. They were not descended from Papa for nothing. They loved the world of ideas, whereas Tom was all practicality. He would smile indulgently as they talked and leave them alone together.

Sometimes she wondered—where did Thomas come from—such a golden boy? She and Tom were so ordinary—oh, especially Tom, she felt that to her shame. Thomas was superior, almost as if he were *His* son.

* * *

Lucy and Sally met for weekends at Ashton as often as possible. It was on a warm day in early summer that Mama greeted them at the door with the happy news that Jenny was to be married.

"That makes me feel so old," Sally moaned.

"I do believe she's captured the very best man in the state, if not the country," Lucy said. "Isn't it grand? She deserves him."

Jenny was to marry Arthur Harrington, a tall, quiet young gentleman. An example of the very best end product that generations of good breeding could produce. Arthur himself was modest, devoted to Jenny. He managed what remained of his family's estates and land. He worked hard and prospered, making sure that his family prospered with him, and later would share generously with Jenny's family.

"I'm afraid I'll not make it down All Saints aisle. Jenny, you should ask Tom to give you away," Papa said a few weeks before the wedding. He was old enough to be Jenny's grandfather and weakened by several heart attacks.

"Oh, no, Papa," Jenny said. "You took all the other girls and you're taking me, too."

So he did, white head erect, step slow but steady. When they reached the front pew, Jenny's groom stepped up to take her arm and Papa sank down beside Mama. But when the rector asked, "Who gives this woman to be married to this man?", Papa rose and said in a voice that reached the back most pew, "I do."

Jenny and Arthur settled nearby on Harrington land right outside of Columbia.

"Jenny has done just the right thing, as usual," Daphne had commented—a trifle sourly, Lucy had to admit.

Papa, as always, had made the final and correct judgment.

"At last," he had said when Jenny told him she was going to marry Arthur. "This time there has arrived a man to whom I can safely entrust the welfare of my wife and daughters."

He was not mistaken in Arthur.

After Jenny's marriage, Papa permitted himself to die.

The community had never seen a funeral such as Papa's. When Mama and her daughters, son-in-laws and grandchildren arrived at the little church, it was full to overflowing with people standing, packed in all the corners. Outside, still others stood bundled up against a harsh wind. A senator was there, a judge, a distinguished Wall Street lawyer, all the way from New York. Those who had crossed Papa's path never forgot him.

"Life without Papa—oh, Lucy," Sally said, "what will we do without him?"

"We have each other, we have Mama. Sally, the longer I live the more I appreciate my sisters. We always have each other."

* * *

The years when the Great Depression gripped the country were not much worse than other years for the Willoughbys. Everyone had to tighten their belts. Poverty was everywhere, almost like Reconstruction days.

Men, sometimes accompanied by women and children, arrived in Columbia, and even Ellerton, hanging on to the sides of the trains that came in, then jumping off into the woods before the train reached the station. There were makeshift camps all through the woods near any railroad tracks. At daybreak, the drifters headed into town where they panhandled on street corners and lined up outside the churches where soup and bread were handed out, and coats and sweaters when winter descended.

Anyone connected with Ashton had never known hunger. Papa had cultivated a vast vegetable garden. Mama and Josephine canned all summer so that garden vegetables could be served year round. Papa's hogs, calves, and chickens provided the best cured, best prepared meats in the area. But

Papa had unusual nutritional ideas. Pork was strictly limited at the Willoughby table, with poultry and fish from the Congaree River being favored.

Often Mama, under Papa's instructions, served only vegetables at the big midday meal. Of course, they always had rice. It was never omitted.

"You know, girls," Papa told this several times a year, "South Carolinians are said to be very like the Chinese. We both eat rice and worship our ancestors."

It had to be said for Papa and Mama that anyone who lived or worked at Ashton had plenty of good food to eat.

Now I know we didn't even understand *real* poverty, Lucy thought.

Ned did his best to keep up Papa's high standards. But somehow the vegetables were no longer so lavish. The grape arbor was declining and Papa's petted peach and apple trees were gone entirely.

Lucy couldn't pass a really hungry looking person without pressing a nickel or dime into his outstretched hand. And Jenny! Even though she and Arthur were feeling pinched, she ran her own private soup kitchen. The Harrington land was close to the railroad tracks and the wanderers soon learned at which back door to knock.

Lucy worked in the soup kitchen of the little Ellerton Episcopal Church. She sent extra lunches to school along with those she prepared for Tom and Thomas. She passed Thomas' clothes along the minute he grew out of them, and it seemed to her and to Tom that he grew overnight.

Oh, she was so proud of him! Surely it was not too vain to bask openly and joyously in the glory of such a son as her Thomas? She felt useful, she stayed busy. She was lucky, she was blessed, she told herself. Over and over this was what she told herself.

A sharp noise startles her awake. Ah, a horn—some rude employee summoning another of the same. She wonders if she has been dreaming or just daydreaming.

Adam, she says his name—is dismayed to realize she spoke aloud: relieved that no one heard her.

After those few weeks with Adam, all she had left of him were the letters. She remembers reading them one last time the day before she moved into this place. Not that she needed to read them. Each word is engraved on my heart, she thinks, and smiles at her extravagantly trite thought. She never wanted her Thomas or his children to find them and speculate. Why worry Thomas, and what business of his was it anyway? His was a different generation. She longs for her own—for her sisters.

Sally

1926

A⊤ ASHTON, SALLY TOOK OVER her girls. No amount of worry could dim the joy she felt in being with them, knowing she was not going to leave them, not now or ever again, Lord willing. Papa improved slowly but steadily.

"I've got to get a job and right away," Sally said to Lucy.

"I know. Tom's been asking around in Ellerton, but the salaries are so low. Maybe you'd better try Columbia."

So, Columbia it was. Mr. Withers contacted a Mr. Clyde Ferguson, who'd been at the University of Virginia with him. Mr. Ferguson was a senior partner of the Ferguson, Smith, Johnson Law Firm. Sally was to be his secretary.

She was glad to learn that Mr. Ferguson was safely married with a houseful of small children. It was a salary she could live on, she and her girls.

She found a small furnished apartment in walking distance of the best of the public schools and they settled in before the school term began.

Sally worked hard and fast. She never minded skipping her lunch break, but she ran—actually ran—home to see her girls in from school and was always back home with them by dark.

And so three years passed.

Then Crawford called. His parole had come through. She met him at the train station. The girls were shy with him at first, but when they reached Sally's apartment, he produced twin dolls from his battered leather suitcase.

"Hop up here," he said, placing a daughter on each knee, "and let's decide on names for these ladies." By the time they had settled on suitable names and made plans for an excursion to Main Street for the following afternoon, the girls were laughing and at ease. They both kissed him goodnight without prompting.

Dear God, let it be all right. They've been through so much.

Crawford spent his mornings talking to various cousins and family friends about possible employment and his afternoons with his daughters, but the interviews yielded no job offers. By the second week Sally began to smell alcohol on his breath when he bent over to give her a welcome-home kiss as she came in from work.

Oh, no, no, I can't go through this again.

Then at the end of the second week, it was Crawford who broached the subject of their future.

"I'm broken, Sally. I know you can see it. I should have blown my brains out before I let myself be put in that place. Did you know that's what your father wanted me to do? He never said anything, of course. But remember the day I came to tell you and the girls goodbye? My last day of freedom? Well I saw his pistol on the shelf in that wardrobe I always use. I checked. It was loaded. I've never seen it left out before. I knew that's what he wanted. It's what he would have done, of course. He would never have let himself be locked away, never have let his family have a member in jail, for God's sake! I guess I was already broken. There was a time when, at least, I wasn't a coward."

Sally didn't try to dispute it. It was too obviously true.

After a long pause, he said, "Sally, you're doing just fine without me. The girls seem happy, so unscarred by it all. I'm not going to be a burden to you. I can at least manage that much. I'm going home—'the place that when you have to go there they have to take you in.'" He gave a little hollow laugh.

It's best, yes, that's best.

Her relief was mingled with regret and sadness— oh, it *was* so sad....

"It's your decision, Crawford," Sally said. "I respect it—and you for making it. The girls have to come first with me now."

So he returned to Tradd Street. Mrs. Carsworth never left the house now. Eloise ventured out only when necessary. Crawford occasionally emerged and took a train, then later when they became available, a bus, to see his daughters. He never forgot their birthdays, or Sally's.

"You should divorce me, Sally," he said more than once. But she refused. She'd insisted on marrying him when everybody knew she shouldn't and she'd taken him on for better or for worse. It had turned out for the worse, all right, but that was not going to make her break her vow. She might be a fool but she was no quitter.

Just as Mama had predicted, Crawford's disgrace had not ruined his girls. They attended the University of South Carolina, living cheaply at home, with tuition being paid by Jenny and scholarships. They joined the Tri Delt Sorority, were presented to society at the Assembly Ball and the Saint Cecilia. Sally breathed great sighs of relief.

When Liz was preparing to graduate from the University, she announced her intention of marrying a Charleston man who was completing law school that same year.

Charleston, again! But other than the accent, Sally could see no resemblance to the Carsworths. Benjamin was bright and had a job in his father's law firm waiting for him. His mother had been a good friend to Sally in her nightmare years.

Sally asked for and received a nice raise in her salary. Lucy and Mary got to work readying Ashton for yet another wedding reception, for where else was home to Liz? Jenny's wedding gift was to finance food, flowers, even music. Mama sewed trousseau lingerie. She was slowing down but not mentally, no indeed, not there. Even Daphne came through. She sent a gorgeous wedding gown in the latest style as her gift to the bride.

The day arrived. The clan had gathered at Ashton. The June day was balmy. Lucy and Sally sat on the big back porch awaiting Crawford's arrival. Liz had insisted that her father take her down the aisle.

"He's done his best by me—Ellie, too. He showed up for all our birthdays and graduations, he brought little gifts. He wrote whenever he was—well—when he could. I'm not going to have him think I'm ashamed of him."

It was growing dark. The wedding was set for eight o'clock. Sally had expected Eloise and Crawford since early afternoon. Something was wrong.

"So help me God, Lucy," Sally said, "if Crawford shows up drunk I'm going to take this old cane of Papa's and knock him into eternity. He will *not* ruin my poor child's wedding."

"He won't, Sally, certainly not. The men will see to him. Tom will take Liz down the aisle. He loves her like a daughter, you know he does. If Crawford doesn't come soon and sober, Tom will do it. Liz will be fine. Please, please don't let yourself be so upset."

Then a car turned into the clearing, a grim-faced Eloise at the wheel. The passenger door opened and Crawford stepped out.

Crawford? Surely not. She hadn't seen him for two years. The elegant frame was diminished and stooped. His classic profile was slack and puffy with yellowed skin. Saffron-yellow fingers held a lighted cigarette. He smiled. Ah, the old smile. Nothing could obliterate the brilliance of that smile.

He swept off his shabby hat and moved swiftly toward her.

"Sally, still so beautiful."

He took her hand and brought it to his lips.

Yes, he really thought her beautiful. Of all the men who'd said it all through the years, probably only Crawford really meant it. *Crawford, oh Crawford.* She reached up and kissed him on his cheek.

"Come on up and put on your tails. Liz is getting ready, you'll be so proud of her. Isn't it lucky that she has your good looks?"

The ceremony and reception then proceeded flawlessly.

When the last guests had gone, Sally said to Lucy,

"These will be our golden years. The nightmare years are over."

* * *

A year after her wedding, Liz gave birth to twin boys. Boys! At last Sally had some males of her very own. She was filled with joy and gratitude.

Ellie stayed on with her mother. She got her bachelor's degree and taught English and French at Columbia High School. She began work on her master's. She seemed content. She had several interested men friends but none seemed to interest her particularly.

Sally worried. Had the terrible years somehow stunted or warped Ellie's emotional growth? Certainly Ellie loved her sister unreservedly and she took great pleasure in caring for the twins when Liz called on her. She had two or three close friends from college, and was a bridesmaid in several weddings. But the men in her life—they seemed to be mostly *friends*.

"Quit worrying about her," Mama said. "Remember, she's part Pendleton. They're quiet, brainy people. Our Ellie has a first-rate mind. Encourage her to finish that master's degree. She should be teaching in a university. Maybe she could go away somewhere to study this summer."

"Mama, we could never manage the money for that."

"Everyone would help."

"Ellie's proud, very proud. I don't think she would take anymore from this family. She loves you all devotedly and she's so grateful to all of you, but she gets her back up if anything financial is offered from even Liz or me."

Shortly after Liz's wedding, Crawford died quietly in his sleep.

Sally was free now, or so she should be, but somehow she didn't feel free. She felt saddened, diminished. Ah, death was so final! Had she harbored some small hope that there might, after all, be a happier ending for Crawford and herself?

Then only weeks after poor Crawford's funeral, Mrs. Carsworth, like Papa, permitted herself to die. So it was over, all over. Well, she'd never cried over spilt milk yet. She'd not start now.

Sally never lacked for suitors but she kept them at bay. Still, she enjoyed the admiration of an old friend, Glen Ludlowe. He was courtly, devoted, undemanding. He took her to parties, out to dinner. His daughters liked her and encouraged the courtship. He worked for the State Archives, a scholarly but unremunerative position. Sally never seriously considered his offers of marriage. She'd had enough emotion. She wanted calmness.

Then December 7, 1941 arrived and nowhere on earth was calm. Benjamin joined the Navy. Liz and her babies followed him all over the United States. Sally rejoiced for Lucy that Thomas was in pre-med and not in service overseas. Mama had now lived to see four wars. She told her daughters with utter conviction that no cause was worth a single young male life. Her obvious suffering, as her grandsons rushed to join the various armed services, distressed her daughters.

Daphne

❦

1928

WHEN DAPHNE RETURNED TO LOUISVILLE, Kevin insisted that she resume a full social life in spite of her father's death. He particularly wanted her to take more part in his "horse" set, the people she found less congenial than any other of her new acquaintances. From Camden days she had felt ill at ease around them. They talked too freely and roughly. Many of them had backgrounds that were uncertain, if not downright unsavory.

"Here's a list for a dinner party we need to give in a week or two," Kevin said. "Maxwell Herzog will be in town."

Her incomprehension must have shown on her face. He became visibly irritated.

"Can't you remember any of these people? He's the best-known trainer in the United States. He'll be traveling with Tot, as usual. Please attempt to take their arrangements with a little savior faire.

What business of ours is their personal life? These sporting people march to a different drummer. No doubt they consider us very dull and bourgeois. Please try."

"I'll certainly try, Kevin, for your sake. But you really must excuse my prejudices. I've had the good fortune to be raised among ladies, gentlemen and servants. I'm unaccustomed to these people who are neither."

She tossed her curls and went over to pick up Annie, who was stirring in her carriage.

Kevin's face softened as he contemplated the beauty of his daughter and wife standing by the window in the fading sunlight.

Still, his ardor was certainly cooling. Oh what a nuisance—was she supposed to cater to a man for the rest of her life? She had assumed marriage would end all that.

She arranged for the party. It was easy enough with Anna's polished staff at her disposal.

"Mother and father have no interest in these people," Kevin had said. "But Christina enjoys them, so ask her and Josh. She'll no doubt drag him along. You two can chat."

Was he being deliberately unpleasant? She looked at him sharply but said nothing.

When the appointed evening arrived, Daphne was entirely pleased with her arrangements. The dining room table was elegant with Chinese porcelains and heavy silver. She'd done the flowers herself with just a little help from Anna.

The night had turned chilly, so a fire crackled in the bright living room where Charles was serving drinks. She herself was in a long, clinging blue gown, grander than any she had owned before. Anna had insisted on buying it for her.

She smiled and circulated, carefully keeping her expression neutral when the oaths or improper words were bandied about. She was gracious to the middle-aged mistress of the rough-edged guest of honor. She was going to do it right if it killed her. She noted that Christina, the reserved and aristocratic Bostonian, seemed quite comfortable with it all. She would indeed have liked to retreat into a corner with Josh, who was mostly silent, but she wasn't about to give Kevin that satisfaction.

Kevin had personally distributed the place cards. So it was at dinner that she first noticed the hard-looking woman on Kevin's left who was devoting herself entirely to the entertainment of her host. She didn't look young, but then the sun and wind weathered the riders so it was hard to tell their ages. Her hair was so black that it, too, was suspect. Her gown was low cut and she leaned toward Kevin, unnecessarily emphasizing the inescapable view. This was no lady. She appeared to have no escort.

"Josh, who's that woman on Kevin's left? I've forgotten her name."

Did Josh look uncomfortable or was she getting foolishly sensitive?

"Her name's Grace McConnell. She's from New York, I think."

"Who's she with down here?"

"She seems to be traveling with Maxwell and Tot. Some great friend of Tot's, I gather. I talked to her over drinks."

Then it was time for her to turn to Maxwell on her right. At least she had the satisfaction of seeing his face light up when she did a little leaning of her own and bestowed upon him her resurrected old flirtatious smile.

* * *

Pleased with the success of her dinner party, Daphne fell back into her routine of meetings and luncheons. But the center of her thoughts and activities was now Annie. The nursemaid was only for those times when Daphne was away from home or badly in need of rest. Daphne delighted in bathing, cuddling, rocking and petting her child. Anna often joined her in these activities.

"I suppose we're spoiling her dreadfully?" Daphne asked.

"Oh, no," Anna replied. "A baby can't have too much love."

The twosome had now become a trio. Kevin's increasingly late hours and out-of-town trips went unnoticed. Annie was filling a place inside her mother that had always been empty. Maybe what she was beginning to feel was contentment? Maybe now at long last she would be content, if not exactly happy.

Spring was giving way to summer, so the Louisville horse season was winding down. Still, Kevin continued his long hours at the stables and racing grounds. He was often late for dinner, but Daphne usually managed to conceal her annoyance at the inconvenience and attempted to entertain him while they ate their warmed-over food. He was increasingly preoccupied and unresponsive.

It was on a Friday that he called at about five o'clock and asked her to cancel their dinner engagement. He would have to be out until nine or so. Once more, she concealed her irritation. After all, she enjoyed an evening alone with her Annie.

Annie had been asleep for hours and Daphne was reading in bed when she realized it was far past nine o'clock. Goodness, it was almost eleven! She scrambled through her bedside phone book until she found the number of the head groom who lived in an apartment above the stables.

"No, Mrs. Worthington, I haven't seen Mr. Worthington since about five o'clock. I couldn't say where he might be. He left in his Ford, as usual."

As usual—five o'clock! Daphne pushed down the horrid thoughts that were surfacing in her mind. She got out of bed and began to pace about. She opened Kevin's closet without having been conscious of her intention to do so. She turned on the closet light and began to go through his coat pockets.

Oh, dear Lord. What am I doing? What have I sunk to? But she systematically reached into the pockets. Then she began on the trousers. Why do the dress things? She reached into the pockets of a pair of old flannels he often wore to the stables that appeared to be recently and carelessly put away. Her hand grasped a folded piece of paper. She was trembling so that she had to steady herself on the bedpost when she opened the paper under the bedside light.

Darling, last night was wonderful. Every time is better than the time before. I can't bear to go home. See you Friday. I'm counting the hours.
—G.

Daphne threw the note down and rushed to the bathroom. She felt not only ill but faint.

No, no. I will not faint. I will not crumble. Oh God, what to do? Was she going to lose everything? How would she live? How could she stand to live—rejected, the object of gossip and pity?

She threw water on her face, took deep breaths. When she felt steadier, she grabbed the note and a coat, slipped on her shoes and headed straight for the nursery. Once more her actions were instinctive rather than deliberate. She picked up Annie and wrapped her in a light blanket. Annie slept heavily on her shoulder. She grabbed her car keys as she passed through the front hall and drove straight to Anna, holding her baby tightly with one arm. She was sobbing by the time she rang the doorbell with a long, insistent push.

Mr. Worthington appeared, followed closely by Charles, who must have dashed from his third floor apartment. Both were in dressing gowns.

Oh, at last something had flustered the unperturbable Mr. Worthington.

"Why, Daphne, what is it? Anna! Anna! Come here!"

Then Anna was there and Daphne fell sobbing into her arms, still clutching Annie.

"Is Kevin ill? Are you or Annie ill? Is *anyone* ill?"

"No, no."

"Charles," Anna said, "please call Susan to come immediately—to come in her robe. Annie must be put to bed. Then put on a kettle for a cup of tea for Miss Daphne and me."

"Come darling," she said to Daphne, "we'll go to the nice room next to the nursery. We'll sort everything out together."

When they were settled on the guest room sofa with their tea, Daphne's sobs subsided. "Oh, Anna, I'm so ashamed of it all. But where can I turn but to you, *his* mother?"

She pulled the note from her pocket and handed it over. Anna read quickly.

"Oh, dear, oh, dear. I can't blame you at all for being upset. But we must sleep on it. We need to hear what Kevin has to say, but not tonight. I have my favorite sleeping pill right here. You must take it, please, darling, you must. I'm with you. You're not alone in this. I'll see to our precious baby. Susan will sleep in with her—there now."

In minutes Daphne found herself between embroidered linen sheets, covered by a cashmere blanket and falling into merciful oblivion.

She roused when she heard loud, persistent knocks on the door, then voices downstairs, but she never fully awoke until Anna appeared with a cup of coffee and freshly squeezed orange juice.

"You look *much* better." She put down the tray and drew back the curtains to reveal a bright sun.

"I sent Beulah over for clothes for you and Annie. She told your help something vague about your becoming frightened in the night—which I had told her and my other people. I've sent Joshua to the office. The fewer people we have meddling the better. You probably heard Kevin last night, beating on the door and shouting. Thank heavens he thought to come straight here. He appeared very distraught."

"I don't want to see him. I will not see him."

"I know how you feel, darling, but you must hear what he has to say for himself. I refused to discuss it. You and he must have some privacy in this."

"No. I won't see him. There's nothing he can say, it's all in black and white. Where *is* the note? It's mine."

"I left it right here in your bedside drawer. Don't think of me as Kevin's mother in this episode. You are like a daughter to me—the girl I never had.

Annie is the joy of my life. I'm your friend, your ally. But you must talk to Kevin. He's your husband, Annie's father. Your mother would tell you the same thing."

"Oh, Mama, Mama. I would be so ashamed for her to know. And my Papa! If he were alive, he'd murder Kevin. I'm going home, Anna. I must go to Ashton."

"You shall, you shall, poor darling. But you've got to see Kevin. It's absolutely your duty. Your father would agree with me."

Daphne knew that to be true, so she ceased to protest.

"When you're dressed and ready, Kevin will come for you. You can go somewhere private to thrash this out. I'll keep Annie."

"No, Anna, tell Kevin I'll see him at five o'clock at our house. He'll have to leave the house now so Annie and I can go home and I can pull myself together. Thank you, Anna, thank you as always."

Back in her home, she somehow got through the day. She took Annie in her carriage on a long, long walk. She played the piano—hard and loud. She couldn't eat or rest or really think. But she thought to hide the note carefully among her personal belongings. Then she bathed and dressed, fixing her hair and face with trembling hands but with as much care as if she were going to a ball.

At the stroke of five she heard Kevin's key in the lock. He looked pale and disheveled and desperate.

Ah, the coward, desperate because he's been caught, not because he's a liar and a cheat.

She turned to face him. Her head held high.

"Daphne—"

She didn't say a word. *He would get no help from her, the cheat.*

"Please forgive me. I beg you to forgive me, I love you, I love Annie. This woman, this episode, it means nothing."

Still she didn't speak.

"You were so occupied with Annie and I—there was so much drinking, so much exposure. I'm so terribly, terribly sorry. I would give anything to undo this."

She said, "So, I'm at fault for being a mother."

"No, no, that's not what I meant." He reached for her. "Daphne, please." She stepped back as though from a viper.

"I told her today. It's over. I'll never see her again. She means nothing to me. For God's sake, Daphne, for Annie's sake, forgive me. It will never happen again. Please say something. Please answer me."

She moved over to the window, her back to him. After a long pause she turned to face him.

"All right, Kevin, here's my answer. I don't know whether I can forgive you or not. I'll need some time. You should understand that the only reason I even consider this, rather than leaving tonight, is because of Annie. She is now my first consideration—what is best for her. You can sleep in the guest room. I need some time to myself."

She also needed her sisters.

* * *

She went to Ashton. She couldn't tell Mama, dear Mama, who was so bravely enduring Papa's death, who conducted herself just as usual, with calmness, and consideration for the comfort of others. She ended by talking to Lucy. Heaven knows Sally had had enough trouble to make her a likely confidante. But Daphne knew Sally despised her—Sally the indomitable, Papa's own child.

Lucy listened carefully before she said a word.

"Daphne, I think Mrs. Worthington is right. It's your duty to try to forgive Kevin. He's Annie's father. We've all got faults, all make mistakes. Kevin's done a terrible thing to you and your marriage, but you've got to honor the for-better-and-for-worse that you promised. I'm sure Papa would advise that, and Mama, too.

"Oh, Daphne, life is hard for us all. If anyone has an easy ride through life, I can't think who it is. Go home and try. You've got your beautiful Annie." Lucy paused, smiled and took her hand in both of hers. "My Thomas will take her to all the South Carolina coming-out balls, just wait and see."

Daphne went home with Lucy's words ringing

in her ears. She tried not to admire Lucy and Sally. But she did, oh, she did. She tried not to be jealous of their love for each other, but she was, oh, she was. Sally would have said you've made your bed, now lie in it. Well, she had and she would.

Back in Louisville, Daphne said, "We'll put this behind us, Kevin, for Annie's sake."

He moved back into their bedroom and they resumed their routines as best they could. Kevin pointedly stayed away from Saratoga that summer, sending the horses with his trainer while he took Daphne and Annie to New England for a month.

* * *

Back in Louisville, as the fall months wore on, Daphne found her spirits steadily lowering. She had always been sure of just one thing—her appeal to the opposite sex. How could this have happened? *Her* husband unfaithful, her one area of unquestioned success now fraught with failure. Wasn't it bad enough to be the middle sister—the nonintellectual sister—ignored by the older girls, not really admired by Jenny, not like Lucy and Lyda and Sally had been.

She struggled through the days. Was she going to sink into depression like Lucy did after Adam died and then her baby? But who would cater to her, come running every day to bolster her through it like the family had done for Lucy? Anna! Certainly Anna tried. She dropped in frequently, suggested little outings and treats.

Then to Daphne's surprise Josh began to come by to visit with her and with Annie. He usually came at five o'clock. He obviously knew that Kevin never came home before six, or more often seven.

"It's so kind of you to fill in this dreary hour for Annie and me," Daphne said. "Please tell Christina I appreciate her lending you to us."

"Oh, she rides until hard dark—usually it's close to eight o'clock. Now that the boys are away at school, it's pretty dreary at our house, too, when five o'clock arrives. You know that Dad has always insisted on a five o'clock closing hour for the plant. 'Men need to be with their families, he says.'"

He blushed and looked down.

So he knows! I wonder how many people in Louisville do know? She felt the hottest shame—to be the object of gossip and pity—how could she bear it? She felt anger competing with the shame. Yes! She'd show them—show Kevin, show Christina, show the whole damn crowd of them!

She turned around, swirling her short skirt around her knees and smiled at Josh.

"It's certainly my gain that you, like myself, would rather be by a cozy fire than riding a horse on a night like this. Let's have a drink. Everything's right here in the sun room."

She turned her hundred-watt smile on him then and called for Ellen to come get Annie.

"Annie can eat her supper while you and I have a cocktail. I'll drink whatever you're having. You bartend."

She sank down on the sofa. When he returned with their highballs, she motioned him to sit beside her.

"Beats riding in this cold wind any day in the week, doesn't it, Josh?" And once more she turned the full wattage of her beautiful smile toward her brother-in-law.

Of course he came back the next night. It was easy, all too easy. When he began to arrive with flowers or a bottle of exceptional wine, it seemed almost like the old days at Ashton. Did Christina know? Well, she hoped so. And Kevin? She was determined he should know. Let him learn what it felt like to be a cuckold. But Anna—oh Anna. She pushed that thought down. She felt better now, more like her old self. That's what counted.

The time came, she knew it would, when he made his first move. It was near Christmas. The fire was burning brightly, the drinks were in hand. He put his down, took hers from her hand and put it down also, then he grasped both her hands in his and looked at her anxiously and intently.

Goodness, he does look just like his father. Oh dear!

"Daphne, I'm falling in love with you. Daphne, please..."

She pulled away, stood up. "No, Josh. This is impossible. Think of the family."

He rose and stood beside her. "I can only think of you." Then he pulled her into his arms and kissed her, holding her tightly while she didn't struggle but didn't exactly respond either. She heard Kevin's key in the door. She responded then, all right, ah, let Kevin see—let him learn what she had learned.

Josh broke away when he heard footsteps, but when Kevin stepped in the room, his face showed that he grasped the essence of the scene. He looked shocked, stunned almost, as he surveyed the cozy setting and the flushed faces and disheveled clothing of his wife and brother.

Daphne smoothed her rumpled curls. "Just in time for our second cocktail and—what we presume to be your first."

Josh, looking thoroughly miserable, indeed almost ill, murmured, "No, must dash, Christina—expecting me." He fled.

The coward. Just like his brother.

She whirled toward Kevin and met his gaze.

"What in hell is going on here—you and Josh!"

"Really nothing much is going on or has gone on, so far."

"For God's sake Daphne—have you lost your mind—some kind of flirtation with my *brother*?"

"Why not pick on someone your own size? Ask Josh what he's had in mind all those evenings he's been kind enough to entertain Annie and me. I would guess it started out of kindness—pity for the deceived wife of the adulterer."

"So you haven't forgiven me, this is revenge—but Jesus, with Josh!"

"He presented himself. I have not yet had to resort to seeking out male attention."

The quarrel lasted most of the evening. In what remained of the night, Daphne lay awake. *What have I done? Anna means more to me than anyone besides my child and my own mother. Yes, more than Kevin. If I get out of this without Anna knowing, so help me God, I'll put Annie first and foremost and never risk my bond with Anna and my mother again. Dear Lord, what would Mama think of me ... and Papa!*

The next morning, Daphne appeared alone for breakfast with Kevin. She sent Annie to the kitchen with Ellen.

"Kevin, nothing really has happened with Josh. I'm sorry I let the flirtation develop as far as it did. I love this family. Anna is like my own mother. Can we call it even—or almost even—and start again?"

He looked up. He looked relieved.

"Yes, Daphne, please. Let's try again. Who do you think knows better than I do your appeal to the opposite sex? We'll put Annie's happiness first, that's what you want, isn't it?

"That's what I want."

* * *

The arrival of the Depression curtailed the lavishness of the stable enterprises although the machinery company seemed to have suffered very little. Daphne passed bread lines when she drove around the city and a desperate man or woman would occasionally knock on her back door, or more often the kitchen door of Anna's imposing home, asking for food or work. The servants were instructed to hand out nourishing food generously. But other than that and the newspaper's blaring headlines, the Worthingtons took very little notice of the cataclysm that was shaking America. The news from Ashton was that all the brothers-in-law and those of the sisters who had jobs were still employed.

Anna set the tone for the Worthington women by curtailing and simplifying her entertaining and by dressing in a more subdued style. This she managed while still looking elegant and having her parties rated among Louisville's most sought after.

In early 1932 Anna suggested a low-key trip to New York for herself and her daughters-in-law.

"We'll stay inexpensively in the Junior League rooms at the Waldorf and I'll treat you girls to a few new clothes. Those long dreary dresses don't appeal much to me, but we can't go around in our short chemises."

Daphne accepted eagerly and Christina declined, as expected.

Oh well, she wears some uniform-looking shirtwaist or some wrong length skirt with a boring blouse whatever the style or season. I'm glad she's not going.

Daphne didn't give voice to these thoughts but her shrug and the exasperated look she gave Anna served just as well.

Daphne loved every minute of the five-day trip.

Thank heavens Anna never learned about Josh and me. Thank heavens for Anna. I would so love to have Mama here, too. She never gets a treat. Anna would ask her in a minute if I suggested it. But of course Mama wouldn't accept. Mama never accepted hospitality that she couldn't reciprocate.

Daphne firmly halted her musings and began to shop with a vengeance. She chose a green wool suit with a long full skirt and a fitted jacket.

Goodness, these styles are all wrong for me. Lucy would look great in this. But Lucy was another one too proud to do much accepting.

For evening, Daphne selected a slinky blue silk with an almost completely bare back and a small train.

Now that's more like it. This suits me right down to the ground!

She chose several afternoon dresses in small prints with belts at the waist and skirts to mid-calf. At least her waist could well stand emphasis.

Then she bought hats with brims. She'd loved those cloches that emphasized her eyes and oval face.

Oh well, it's more important to stay in style.

She and Anna went to the Metropolitan Museum one afternoon and to the Ziegfeld Follies one night.

They ate fine food, drank special wines. Daphne loved every minute.

"Anna, darling, thank you, thank you," Daphne said when they reached home. "You are my fairy godmother, *not* my mother-in-law."

"Well, you're my own daughter. Just what I would have ordered if I had had the chance."

* * *

During the thirties, Daphne became increasingly immersed in Annie. If she herself didn't quite realize that she was living vicariously through her beautiful child, other people did. Annie had the best of everything—schools, camps, music, dancing, horseback riding. This was to be expected, of course, and being well-endowed, she performed well.

Every summer the Willoughby sisters convened at Ashton, making an effort to overlap visits for at least a week so that the first cousins could know each other—blood kin must know each other, must stand together, always.

A hierarchy existed with the cousins just as it had with the sisters. Lyda's three handsome grownup sons elicited admiration and respect, as did Sally's two pretty girls. Jenny's babies were regarded as brief diversions by some, a nuisance by others. That left Annie and Thomas to fit in where they could. Annie greatly admired her big athletic cousin, who in his turn admired the older Carsworth girls.

Daphne, ever mindful of any possible slight to her darling, noticed and resented this.

But Annie, herself, seemed quite comfortable in any situation. "Come *on*, Thomas," she would say. "I'm waiting for you to go riding with me."

She was accustomed to having her wishes granted. Thomas was accustomed to pleasing others. So off they would go, with Annie satisfied as usual.

Mama, although aging visibly, still was keenly aware of all that occurred with her brood of children and grandchildren. More than once she commented to Daphne, "Remember, dear, the old adage, 'There's nothing so wholesome for a child as a little judicious neglect.'"

Daphne, as always, turned a deaf ear to her parent's advice.

Lucy

Ellerton 1941

A<small>FTER</small> T<small>HOMAS'</small> <small>TRIUMPHANT HIGH SCHOOL</small> career, there was a full college scholarship and to Duke, no less! When World War II began, Thomas was made a private in the U.S. Army, put in uniform and left at Duke to complete his pre-med and medical studies.

Thomas, safe from German or Japanese guns—this was Lucy's special gift from the same providence that had denied her so much. Thomas fretted and wanted to go fight but he stuck it out, probably for her sake.

America had been at war for three months when Tom stepped out of character and presented Lucy with a shock.

It was not just that he surprised her. He presented her with a fait accompli and this he had never done before. He had always consulted her. She advised and consented before he made even the smallest decision.

On this particular chilly evening, as soon as Tom came in from school, he built a big fire. When bright flames were lighting the living room and lifting Lucy's spirits, he poured himself a good-sized portion of bourbon whiskey. He persuaded Lucy to have a pale and very watered down version of the same.

"Sweetheart," he began, "I've joined the Army. It's all set. After thirteen weeks training I'll get the rank of captain that I had at the end of the first war."

He looked happy, transformed. *Yes he was transformed. Of course he'd had his own disappointments—only a high school teacher!* She felt ashamed. She should have noticed more.

"Well—Well, Lucy?"

"Tom," she paused, took a deep breath and then went on, "Tom, I can see you're happy about this. I'm sort of shocked and anxious, of course, but— it's *fine!* You deserve to have what you want. I'm pleased for you. After all, fighting is what South Carolinians do best!" She laughed and he joined in. He drank another bourbon then insisted on taking her to the Ellerton Hotel for dinner. Sitting across the candle lit table, Lucy thought what a good-looking man he still was. *I don't think about that often enough. I've never thought about him hard enough or often enough and now—now he could be killed!*

"Do you know any details yet?" Where will you go first? When can I join you?"

His beaming face lit up still further. He reached across to cover her slim hand with his big one.

"You mean you want to come with me? You'll follow me around anywhere in the country? Is that what you're saying, Lucy?"

Dear Lord, what sort of wife was she that he could doubt that?

"Of course I'm coming with you!"

"I should get my orders a few days from now. After the thirteen weeks initial training period, wives can come. We'll have quarters with the other officers. Maybe I'll land in a place you'll like."

"It'll be an adventure wherever it is. We'll not even think about overseas or—or danger."

"Thank God you're taking it like this Lucy. You know how I hate seeing you distressed. But I just had to do it. I loved the Army. Might have stayed in except—well, no need to go into all that—all behind us and forgotten. I couldn't leave you, Lucy, not when I had a second chance to get you. Was worth it, too." He smiled and released her hand.

Medium-rare steaks had been delivered to their table by their waitress, Sue, who was a former pupil of Tom's. Tom took a moment to fill Sue in on the cause for the celebratory dinner. Acquaintances seated at a nearby table overheard and came over to offer congratulations, thus the evening concluded happily.

Later, when they were preparing for bed, Tom said, "I should've known you'd understand—same background, same sort of rearing. We both know that honor, duty, country—those old-fashioned values mean everything to our kind of people. Couldn't live with myself if I didn't do my part."

"I know, Tom, I know and of course I understand. I'm proud of you. Thomas will be too." *Proud but mostly envious.* But she would never say that and neither would Thomas.

As it turned out, Tom received his training at Fort Benning in Columbus, Georgia, and then was stationed there in the cadre that trained incoming inductees.

Lucy arrived as soon as allowed, which was just in time to receive the full force of South Georgia heat. Well, she was used to that. She settled into the small house allotted to a captain. She was certainly accustomed to that also and she proceeded to convert the house into a home. Much as Sally and Crawford had done in the first World War, Lucy and Tom reached out to other couples, welcomed into their home the officers who were without wives and they were warmly received in return. Tom seemed to have reconciled himself to the fact that his age and lack of long-time army experience would disqualify him for combat. He obviously enjoyed working with the raw recruits. Lucy was happy to see him enjoying his new role.

There was, indeed, a new zest to their lives with the change of venue and exposure to people from all over the country.

Ah, but the uniforms, the wartime atmosphere, the occasional New Englander she encountered— the old, old wound in some way freshened. She fought down the memories. Once she met a man who had been at Harvard at about the right time. But she was never in his presence without Tom. She couldn't ask if he had known *Him*, not in front of Tom. *His* name was never ever mentioned except once in a while she talked about *Him* to Sally. She missed Sally and Mama and Thomas, oh how she missed her Thomas! But she and Tom could afford long distance calls now and they spoke to him each week.

A few days after the Allied Victory in Europe, Thomas received his medical degree along with a commission as a 2nd Lieutenant. He had a two week leave before he would depart for Germany and the Army of Occupation.

Tom was still hard at work training troops who, presumably, would fight in Japan. So alone, Lucy joined Thomas for his graduation and his leave.

Ah, this was a time to be treasured, and she savored every moment. A secondhand Ford, the best that could be found around Columbus, was Thomas' graduation gift. Lucy had saved gas coupons. She and Thomas drove from Durham to Ellerton where he contacted old friends—mostly female—the men were in service.

It will be a change from those nurses at Duke. Lucy had thought them to be a very aggressive lot but had wisely refrained from saying so.

They visited Ashton, of course. Mary and Ned and, most especially Mama, were so very happy to see Thomas. Sally and Ellie came from Columbia.

"It's a mini-family reunion," Thomas said. "When this is all over, we'll have a real reunion—the Wilmington cousins, the Louisville group—everybody. Grandmama, you can count on it."

Mama beamed.

"I shall see that I remain alive for that occasion—not much to look forward to at my age—but my family together and safe—that's worth staying around for."

Then, in August, Tom's military career ended. With Japan's surrender, the training of new troops came to a halt. Lucy and Tom packed up and headed back to Ellerton.

Tom returned to the classrooms and playing fields of Ellerton High School. Lucy picked up her friendships and former activities. Neither acknowledged to the other any feelings of disappointment, of expectations unmet, ambitions unfulfilled.

Lucy, as before, lived vicariously through Thomas.

She saved his letters. After sharing them with

Tom, she then poured over them alone, reading between the carefully constructed lines that his free time was not all devoted to sightseeing and culture. She was happy for him. She wanted him to live in a way that she had not.

* * *

When all wartime hostilities had ceased and the Willoughby households were rejoicing at the survival of their particular servicemen—then and only then—almost as if she were following Papa's example, Mama died. It was a peaceful death. She drifted away while asleep in the very bed in which she had been born. Mary found her and, just as she had done for a lifetime, she quietly assumed her responsibilities. She called the sisters and cousins, made all arrangements and readied Ashton for an onslaught.

The Willoughby daughters, accompanied by husbands, children and grandchildren, quickly gathered at Ashton. Bedrooms, living rooms, the huge hallways were full.

"Why did we have to wait until darling Mama's death to get together in such force?" Sally said. "She would have loved every minute of a gathering like this."

"I'm so thankful she lived to see all the boys come home," Jenny said. "Have you ever known anyone to hate war so much? She was overjoyed when I had two girls."

Mary said, "She didn't seem to mind that I had no children." She sighed, "Well, I minded, but I guess I was too old when I married. I can't blame Ned. He spent years trying to make me decide. I had such trouble making decisions.

"Mama certainly loved all of us and showed it in every way, but maybe raising six girls with Papa being such a prima donna was harder than she ever admitted."

Lucy whispered to Sally. "I'm just grateful she survived us. Lyda doesn't look well at all."

"It's sad that some of the men are gone," Sally said, "Lyda's James, and of course my poor Crawford."

"All of you in South Carolina are so lucky to be close to each other," Daphne complained. "Lyda and I are cut off, especially me—way out in Kentucky."

The sisters would miss Mama to the end of their lives, but they had each other.

Oh, thank heavens, we have each other. Surely they were all thinking the same thing.

* * *

In due course Thomas returned and went to Charleston to complete his medical training in obstetrics. He'd been there several months when he called Lucy late one Sunday night.

"Thomas, is anything wrong?"

"No, no Mother, just the opposite—I'm wondering if I could bring a girl home with me this coming weekend?"

"Of course, Thomas, who is she?"

"Alice Sorrenson, her parents know Aunt Sally. We'll get in sort of late Friday—after supper—and stay through Sunday midday dinner. How's that sound?"

"Wonderful, your father and I will kill the fatted calf."

Lucy and Tom were waiting on the porch when Thomas drove into the driveway Friday night. Lucy watched him open the car door, leaning his dark head close to the still darker one of the slim girl he was escorting in, his hand protectively closed on her elbow.

This is the one. Dear Lord, let her be right for him.

When the two of them reached the light of the porch and Thomas began the introductions, his eyes flew straight to Lucy. She smiled and stepped forward, putting her arms lightly around Alice.

"Welcome to Ellerton, what a treat Thomas is giving us."

Lucy was not mistaken. This was the one. Six months later Thomas married his Alice.

It was to Lucy's everlasting credit that when that time came, she turned him loose. With both hands, with her whole heart, with nothing held back, she set him free to love another woman best and to live another life with herself as a minor player. Her friends marveled at such largeness of spirit. Everyone knew Thomas had been the joy of her life. But then her friends had no way of knowing what Lucy was capable of when she really loved.

It was a different world that Thomas came home to. In his quiet way, Thomas participated in the changes. He and Alice not only danced at the St. Cecilia Ball but worked for the Chamber of Commerce and the United Way. He and his partners in obstetrics made very good money. Thomas and Alice bought a fine new house near the new country club. They played golf, they traveled, their sons went to Porter-Gaud private school and to camp in North Carolina. Their daughter was enrolled at Ashley Hall.

It was a good time for Lucy. She and Tom drove to Charleston and stayed with the grandchildren when Thomas and Alice traveled. She saw her sisters regularly. She was always available when her help was needed in any of their households.

Sally and Lucy spoke on the telephone several times a week. Lucy felt that Sally's life and family were in someway hers as well.

"It's symbiosis," Sally said. "That new term could have been invented for us."

"Yes," Lucy replied. "We love the others. Think what Jenny means to us and Mary. But—well..."

They seldom spoke of such things. Between them words were not really necessary, but how words flowed between them!

"We're Papa's children," Lucy said. "Words both written and spoken are what we live by."

"Those black eyes of Papa's would flash fire if he could see that phone bill poor Tom Thornton pays every month." Sally laughed and Lucy joined in.

She smiles to herself but keeps her eyes tightly closed. She pictures Sally's face. She wonders if her thoughts are somehow reaching Sally. Only with Sally could she talk freely about Adam.

Oh Sally—silently in her head and heart she is speaking to her sister . . .

I never danced with Him. If I could have had one waltz, his hand on my waist, his other hand clasping mine, the two of us whirling, whirling to Danube So Blue.

We never ate a meal together—His face, that handsome face reflected in flickering candlelight. She concentrates fiercely—imagining, imagining.

Sally

THROUGHOUT THE WAR YEARS, Ellie had continued to teach. Her students adored her and emerged from Columbia High School so well prepared in English and French that the professors at the University and Clemson had begun to realize that something special existed in those departments at Columbia High.

"You're getting a *reputation*, Ellie," Sally said. "Now cash in on it and try to get funding so you can concentrate on your master's."

"Well, maybe I will," Ellie answered. "Twenty-seven is not old nowadays, mother. I love my pupils, I'm contributing something important—at least I think so."

"Of course you are. Nothing's more important than helping young minds to develop. I wish Papa were here to talk to you on that subject."

"You're thinking about men, mother. I just don't love the company of men like you do. And I notice you don't seem very eager to take on marriage either."

Some months after Mama's death, Ellie began to complain of headaches.

"Lie down, Ellie, take an aspirin, you work too hard." Sally spoke cheerfully enough, but she felt anxious. Ellie wasn't one to complain about ordinary aches and pains.

A few weeks later, Ellie walked into the living room where Sally was seated reading the newspaper. She staggered slightly, then steadied herself against the door frame.

My God, like Crawford.

But of course it wasn't that. Ellie, like Liz and Sally, was afraid of alcohol, never drank.

"You'd better see a doctor about those headaches," Sally said. "There may be something very simple you can take or do. Please, Ellie."

Then, just a few nights later, Ellie said, "Something's wrong with my eyes. I seem to see two of everything."

"All right, Ellie, do I call Dr. Edgerton or do you? He has to see you right away."

He did. Sally came home early to be there when Ellie got back from her appointment.

"He's having me see a Dr. Willingham, who's had neurological training. Ten o'clock tomorrow." She tried to sound matter-of-fact but Sally could see that she was frightened.

"I'll go with you."

"No, mother, don't start taking time off from work and all that. The doctor is working me in, it'll be a long wait."

It was agreed that they would meet at the apartment at lunchtime.

Sally was waiting when she heard Ellie's key in the lock. One look at her face and she knew it was serious.

"What, what? Tell me quickly."

"Mother..." Ellie closed her eyes for a moment, then opened them. "It's bad. Doctor Edgerton thinks it's a brain tumor."

Oh merciful God. Sally felt her own vision blur. Her chest constricted as if in a vise. She grasped the back of a chair. *Help me God! Help me hold up for my Ellie.*

"Darling Ellie," she took a deep breath, "we're not going to panic." Sally was surprised to find that her voice was normal, even firm. "We'll fight this thing, we'll beat it, you'll see."

"Money," Ellie said.

Sally put her arms around Ellie. She'd been aching to hold her. "Don't worry. That's not your worry. Jenny and Daphne will help. We've got Lucy and Thomas. We've got to call Thomas. He'll know if we should see other doctors and which ones."

"I'm going to call Liz now." Ellie broke away and went to the phone in the hall.

My God, my God, oh, Mama, Papa. Sally felt so alone, so very alone.

Liz drove up the next day. Thomas called—Liz had already telephoned him. Yes, they should see another doctor.

His own school, Duke, had the finest neurological department this side of Johns Hopkins. He knew the head man. He would make appointments. Time was important. They must get ready and go as soon as he called them. Lucy came from Ellerton, ready to stay for as long as Sally wanted her.

"Don't worry about money," Jenny said. "Arthur and I will see to that. That is what families are for."

Daphne called from Louisville. "Sally, this is something I can do for you at last. Kevin and I will fly Ellie anywhere in the world. She must have the best. Are you completely satisfied with Duke?"

"Oh, yes, Daphne, and everybody's helping, but thank you." Sally found that kindness brought her closer to tears than anything. But she never succumbed, not once.

Daphne didn't pursue the subject, but a large check arrived by special delivery the next day.

And the gift was to prove a godsend, relieving Sally of any further concern about medical bills.

Sally, Lucy, Liz, and Ellie had two days of waiting in Columbia.

Sally felt paralyzed with fright. At Ellie's insistence she went to work. She thought perhaps the sisters wanted time alone together. So she forced herself to leave them and Lucy took herself off to Jenny's. Sally organized her office affairs for her absence, but it all seemed dreamlike, not real.

When she came home the first evening, appreciably earlier than usual, her small living room was crowded with young men and women. The word had spread rapidly among Ellie's friends and there was a rallying around that seemed to lift Ellie's spirits.

Sally tried not to hover, but it was hard to tear her gaze away from Ellie.

Dear Lord, help my Ellie. What is she feeling? How can I help her? If only Ellie would let down, permit herself to cry and rage against a cruel and unjust Providence. But no, she maintained her remarkable composure.

The next day, when Sally arrived home, she found Ellie alone in the living room with a big hulking boy and a small pretty girl.

Ah, students!

After the introductions, Ellie said, "Joanne is here representing my French class and Peter is from my Senior English class. Look at the beautiful gifts they brought."

They were indeed lovely gifts—a lacy bed jacket, a big bottle of White Shoulders perfume and a copy of *All the King's Men* by Robert Penn Warren. Apparently this new novel was Peter's choice and the contribution of those members of the football team who had taken Ellie's Junior and then Senior English.

It took all Sally's social skills to effect the departure of the guests. For a while there she thought they might stand in the doorway until dawn. Then just as he started away, the big blonde boy turned back again.

"Miss Carsworth," he paused.

Good heavens, his blue eyes were brimming with tears.

"I hate that I gave you so much trouble last year." He paused again and Ellie stepped closer.

"Now Peter, you weren't all that bad."

"Miss Carsworth," he pressed on. "I'm glad you were strict with our crowd. I'm glad you *made* us learn. If I amount to anything, I guess I'll owe it mostly to you."

His tears spilled over. Ellie put her arms around his considerable bulk. He hugged her tight for a moment then blundered through the doorway with Joanne at his heels.

"Ellie, darling Ellie, what a tribute."

Sally crushed her daughter to her and at last, at last, they both cried.

The next morning Liz drove Sally, Lucy and Ellie to Durham. Thomas would come when he heard from the surgeon.

Sally was dismayed when she saw Duke Hospital—huge, bustling, arrows drawn on floors to direct traffic, numbers issued, loudspeakers blaring, no one appearing to be personally known to anyone else. Ellie grew more and more silent.

Our Father who art in heaven, Sally tried to pray. *Merciful God, oh help my child.* She felt pure terror.

Yes, it was a brain tumor. But X-rays indicated that it was in an operable spot and surgery would take place on Wednesday. The great man would do it himself.

Thomas came. He would go into the operating room with Ellie, stay with her the whole time. His presence was a balm.

Oh, thank you, God, for Thomas.

Liz had to leave the room when the nurse began to shave Ellie's head the night before the operation. But Sally and Thomas sat right there.

"Good thing you've got the perfectly shaped head and the flat ears of your handsome father," Sally said. Strange, she thought, this is the first time I've thought of Crawford.

"What does it matter? We're going to get you a red wig." Thomas managed a small joke.

Then the nurse made them leave. It was time for Ellie's sleeping pill. The operation was scheduled for six a.m. the next day.

"Much the best time to get," Thomas said. "The surgeon, the assistants and nurses, everybody, are all fresh. That's when they do their best work."

Thomas, Sally, Liz, and Lucy, huddled together in the nearby hotel, tried to eat. They held up for each other. At five o'clock the next morning they were in Ellie's room.

"Okay, gang," Thomas said, "clear out now. Ellie and I are going to get this show on the road."

At six o'clock Sally said, "I'm going to the chapel.

I'm going to pray." Liz and Lucy went with her. She tried to pray. She knelt. But in her head there was only *oh God, oh God, oh please, oh please. Was that a prayer? Was there a God?*

They went back to the place Thomas had told them to wait. It was actually four hours but it could have been four days or one hour. Sally was numb. She simply sat.

The great surgeon was coming toward her, his green mask pushed down, his face tired, stern.

Oh God, my God, please, please.

"We got most of it, couldn't get it all. It's malignant. Can't give you much encouragement. Must simply wait and see. Everything possible has been done. She sustained the operation very well." He was gone.

But Thomas was there. He put one arm around Sally and the other around Liz. His mask was on his chest, his face drawn.

"Now, Aunt Sally, we'll have to wait and see. The operation went well, very skillfully done. Ellie's vital signs are good. One never knows about these brain operations. She'll be in recovery several hours. Let's go get a Coke, I'll check on her soon."

Dear God, thank you for Thomas.

At last they rolled Ellie into her room.

Oh, my Ellie!

Her head was swathed in bandages. Her face was as white as the bandages. Her chiseled profile, Crawford's profile, stood out clear and beautiful.

Ellie, Ellie, heal, heal, live, live. Heal her God, heal her. Let her wake. Wake, Ellie, wake.

Sally sat by the bed, took Ellie's cold hand gently into both of hers.

"You must leave now. The patient needs quiet." The nurse's voice was without warmth, not human.

"Her mother and I will stay for a few minutes," Thomas said.

Oh God, thank you for Thomas.

But Thomas had to leave the next day. His own patients were waiting, frantic that some other doctor might have to deliver their babies, perform their hysterectomies.

The three women took turns sitting with Ellie. It was difficult for Liz and Lucy to get Sally to move from the bedside, but when Liz stayed she would leave for brief snacks, short rests. A thick fog enveloped her. The only moments that were not torment were those spent sitting by Ellie.

Oh please, God, please. Live, Ellie, live.

Sally sat. Days passed. Every day that Ellie remained unconscious was a day lost and was making recovery less likely.

Wake, wake, please, please...

It had been six days. Hope was fading.

Darkness fell early on the seventh night. A heavy rain began to fall. It was late January, winter. Sally had always hated winter. She loved sun and light. The nurses had insisted that they leave at eleven o'clock each night.

"Go home and rest," Thomas said on the phone. "The eleven to seven nurses are always the best."

Lucy and Liz prepared to leave. "I'll just stay a little longer. Liz can come for me when I call her," Sally said.

Maybe it was midnight, Sally didn't know the hour, when a tall, imperious-looking nurse came in and found Sally still there, in her chair by Ellie's bed.

"You will have to leave now, Mrs. Carsworth. Those are our rules. We can't make exceptions."

Sally turned burning eyes on the tight, closed face of the nurse. Her voice was low but hard.

"I'm not leaving, *you* are. No power in this hospital or on the face of the earth can move me from this room. That's my *child* in that bed. I was there when she was born and I'll be here when she dies. Get out, stay out, don't you or anyone else dare open this door again."

She went back by the bed and took Ellie's white, transparent hand into both of hers. The rain beat on the windows and Ellie's breath came in harsh rattles. Otherwise, there was no sound.

She put her face down by the pillow and whispered, "I'm right here Ellie, I'm right here. I love you, my baby, I love you. May God make his face to shine upon you, Ellie. May God give you peace, that peace that passeth all understanding, my Ellie."

The harsh breaths stopped. There was a terrible stillness.

Dear God, watch over her. Surely there is a God? Mary, Mother of Jesus, be with my child. Angels surround her. Surely there are angels?

She put her head back down by Ellie's. She didn't move. She hardly breathed.

Please take me, God. Oh, surely there's a God who'll take me too?

She had no idea how much time passed. Then the door opened slowly, quietly. It was Liz and Lucy.

"It's over," Sally said.

Liz sank down on the bed and put her arms around her dead sister and began to sob. But Lucy went straight to Sally, enfolding her in her arms and holding her tight.

"Oh, Sally, Sally."

* * *

Sally turned to stone, inside and out she was stone. "Shock," people murmured. She didn't cry. Everybody else did. It continued to rain. Tears and rain, people bringing flowers, bringing food. Food! Why did they bring all that food? Liz collapsed and Benjamin rushed up to be with her. His family took over their boys.

Lucy stayed in Columbia with Sally. She wouldn't leave. She brought cups of tea and stood until Sally drank. She loosened Sally's clothes and pressed her down to the bed, then put herself down beside her. Sally walked out in the rain, Lucy ran up to walk beside her, opening an umbrella over both their heads.

It was still raining the afternoon they buried Ellie, in the ancient churchyard of All Saints, close by Mama and Papa. Rain beat on the canopy above Sally's head. She held Liz's hand, Benjamin put an arm around each of them. The young rector from Trinity Church in Columbia came to join the old preacher from All Saints. They spoke their words but she didn't hear them. She fastened her eyes on the huge oak tree that guarded the graves. Moss hung heavy from its branches. Why was there moss in all the tress around here? Moss this far from the coast? Yes, Sally had turned to stone.

Back in Columbia, Lucy stayed. Liz had to leave. Her boys were becoming visibly upset. After a week had passed Sally got up, put on her navy blue suit and went to work. The lawyers, young and old, the other secretaries were kind, solicitous. She needn't feel that she had to come in every day. She must take as much time off as she needed. She scarcely heard them. She was a stone.

But she could work and her hands flew over the typewriter. She insisted on taking Mr. Ferguson's dictation herself. She had been promoted to a sort of office manager. She hired and supervised the other secretaries.

Sally walked home. Lucy had a hot meal ready

when she came in at dark. Wind or rain, and on the sunny, sparkling day that finally arrived, she walked and walked.

She looked across the table at Lucy, and her vision cleared a little. For the first time she really focused on the anxious face opposite her.

"You've got to go home, Lucy. Tom needs you."

"Do you want me to leave, Sally?"

"Yes. I've got to be alone."

Lucy looked desperately anxious now.

Sally got up and looked out the window. Outside there was blackness.

"I know what you're worried about. But I'm not going to do it. Of course it would be a relief beyond description to just become oblivious, to end this. A gun, a knife, a jump from the highest floor of the Jefferson Hotel, any of them would be easy, easy."

She came and sat back down. Lucy's big eyes were enormous now, never leaving Sally's face.

"Here's why I'm not going to do it. I'm not going to give those goddamned demons or devils or whatever forces have been pursuing me most of my life the satisfaction, that's why. I will not break."

She rose again and began to pace. Lucy got up and paced beside her, step for step. Up and down the little room they walked.

"What kind of God would let a thing like this happen, would cut down a beautiful, brilliant young girl, a girl, good through and through? Who wants a God like that?"

She raised her fist and whirled back to the dark window.

"Damn you all to hell," she said to the blackness outside. "I will not break."

The next day Lucy left. Who knew better than she that when Sally had determined on a course, that was it?

Now Jenny came by each late afternoon. One day the young rector from Trinity arrived just after the sisters had removed their coats.

Of course, Jenny had called him, Sally smiled. Poor Jenny, trying everything.

Jenny left them alone. She would make tea for them all, she said.

Dr. Smithers was a quiet man and he sat quietly beside Sally, not trying to make conversation. As for Sally, she was stone.

Finally he said, "I'm praying for you, Mrs. Carsworth, every day. More people than you can possibly know are praying for you."

"Thank you."

"I wish I could help you. I can't, but this much I know. The God I believe in will help you. You may not feel it now, but help will come. Our prayers for you are that help will come. They'll be answered."

She sat like the stone that she was.

After the tea had been drunk, he stood to leave. When Jenny went for his coat and hat, he put his hand on Sally's head and held it there for a few moments.

"God have mercy on Sally, Your child, who has had such deep and terrible trouble. Walk beside her, help her carry this grievous load. I ask it in the name of the Son You lost, just as she has lost her daughter. Amen."

She looked at his clerical collar while he spoke, that backwards collar that had symbolized comfort as long as she could remember. She liked the feel of his hand on her head.

When the door closed behind him, she began to cry. Jenny put her arms around her and they cried together.

* * *

Spring came early that year. All Columbia turned into a garden. Azaleas, pink, red, white, ran together in great clumps up and down the streets. Fruit trees and dogwoods opened their delicate buds above them.

Lucy came with her suitcase and Sally laughed.

"Come on in and be your sister's keeper, your favorite role."

"My absolute favorite." Lucy hugged her tight.

After a few days, again over a hot evening meal Lucy had prepared, she said, "Liz needs you, Sally. She's very, very shaken by Ellie's death. She and Ellie were the closest sisters in the world." Her eyes met Sally's. She smiled, "Well, I take that back, they were the second closest sisters in the world."

Sally said, "Never think I don't appreciate you, Lucy, just because I don't say it. What would I do without you?"

"I don't intend to let you find out," Lucy said. "I'm sticking with you and that's that." They both smiled.

"You can serve a real purpose if you move to Charleston. We know what families can mean to each other. These are important years for Liz. She needs you to stand behind her. The boys need to be with you. Generations have a lot to give to each other. You'll be right there for my Thomas. It's hard for me to urge this because you'll be further from me, but I know it's right."

"Yes, of course it's what I should do. I may feel a hundred years old but I'm only forty-nine. There may be a long haul ahead and I must try to be useful to the end. I'll set the wheels in motion."

"Oh, don't disturb her."

Of course she is disturbed and it's not her Thomas this time. She keeps her eyes closed, her head down but she listens.

"Mrs. Thornton seems to sleep more each day. But we see that she eats and gets her fresh air!"

What a patronizing bore the nurse is. Her poor visitors. She listens carefully.

"She was so lovely—my favorite aunt."

It's Jenny's girl! She chides herself for thinking of someone over sixty-five as a girl. Well, why not? They're all boys and girls to her.

She thinks how kind of Jennifer to come. But it must be late in the day because she is tired—much too tired to make the effort to converse.

"Anyway, Susan, I want you and my other grandchildren to know your great-great aunt.

She's the last of that generation. It was a different world she and my Mother lived in—closer to "Gone With the Wind" than the South we lived in now."

She suppresses a smile. It's different all right! The old-fashioned virtues—duty, honor—who speaks of such things now? She's glad Papa and Mama never lived to see the level of behavior that prevails.

Daphne

❦

As the years passed, Kevin and Daphne maintained their marriage but lived more and more separate lives. Their headstrong daughter was now the usual subject of any conversations they engaged in when alone. While Kevin followed his horses, Daphne had remained at home with Annie. She no longer cared what he did or with whom, so long as he behaved with discretion and did nothing to embarrass her or more important, Annie.

The beginning of World War II ended life as the Willoughbys and Worthingtons had known it, just as it did for families all over the world. Daphne's primary concern was its effect upon Annie's life.

Pretty, bright and every bit as spoiled as Mama had predicted, Annie departed for college in the fall of 1944. Sweet Briar had been her parents' choice, and since this happened to appeal to her, as well, she took herself off, burdened with enough clothes to supply an entire dormitory.

Daphne, deprived of her life's work, lived for Sunday evening telephone calls from Annie. The thunderbolt came one Sunday in early October.

"Mother," Annie said, "I've got some very important news. I've met the man I'm going to marry."

"Good heavens, Annie. Are you joking? Tell me about this person."

"This person is Captain Bartrum Young of the United States Air Corps. He's wonderful—tall, handsome, smart—a West Point graduate. His father's a General in the Army, he's a West Point man, too."

"Where are they from? Are they southerners?"

"*From*—I just told you, mother, they're several generations of West Point men, regular Army. They're from everywhere. Bart has lived all over the world."

"You must bring him home at Thanksgiving."

"Mother," Annie said, an edge of impatience in her voice. "Bart's been in the European Theater. He's flown all the missions allowed. He's at Langley Air Base now. He's been here a year and he's volunteered for more combat missions. He'll get orders any time. We've got to be prepared to get married anytime, anywhere."

"Annie, dear, please. You just met this man, you're only eighteen years old, this is insane!"

"Mother, I've made up my mind, just tell Father and Grandmother."

Daphne consulted with Kevin.

"It's impossible," Kevin said. "You've got to forbid this."

"You should be the one to do so. You're her father."

Kevin made no reply. They both knew Annie had never been forbidden anything.

They set out for the big house to inform Anna. Mr. Worthington had died several years ago, but Anna continued her life as usual. Her large staff, aged and slowed, remained with her, perhaps because of their declining energies and abilities.

When they had explained the situation, Anna said, "You and Kevin should go to Virginia, next weekend if possible, and meet this young man. Maybe you can arrange an airplane flight or the train. You can drive if necessary, I have plenty of gas coupons for you to use."

"If only traveling weren't so difficult," Daphne said. "But our cars are in good shape and I've got most of my ration of gas left too. Let's drive."

When they reached Lynchburg the next weekend and checked into the only available hotel room, they were exhausted. But both parents exerted every effort, as they always did when Annie was concerned, and managed to appear at their best when they met the young couple in the hotel lounge.

Bart was indeed good-looking, articulate, sophisticated. He was twenty-six years old and an only child, he said. Both parents were children of Army officers. Home? Why, any Army base was home to him.

Daphne abandoned hope of his ever understanding the sense of place and home inbred in any southerner. But Annie was so young! And she hardly knew this man. Oh, Annie must marry the right man—surely *someone* could manage to marry the right man? Please God, let it be my Annie.

The young couple were adamant. Bart's father, General Young, and his mother were in San Francisco. Bart expected to be sent to the Pacific Theater. Orders might come any day. They would marry in Virginia, Washington, or the West Coast. It seemed unlikely that they could manage Kentucky if they were to have any time together before his departure for the Far East.

Stunned and defeated, Daphne and Kevin drove home to await developments.

Bart's orders came on November 1st. He was to report to Hamilton Field in one month.

"It's near Sausalito, mother," Annie said. "That's a beautiful spot in California, on the water, perfect for a honeymoon—then there's San Francisco! I've always, always wanted to see San Francisco. Bart should have at least a month at Hamilton getting indoctrination and so forth. That gives us two months together.

"Can you come right away and help me get a wedding dress and some gorgeous lingerie? That's all I need. I've got all these new clothes we bought for school."

Annie paused and caught her breath, then rushed on, "General Young can arrange a plane to take us all to the West Coast. Tell Grandmother she has to come, too."

Daphne was trembling with emotion but kept her voice steady.

"I'll talk to Kevin and Anna and call you later, darling. I want you to be happy, that's all I want or will ever want—your happiness."

When Anna, Kevin, and Daphne were seated in Anna's living room over drinks, Daphne hardly heard what the others were saying—the objections, the reservations, the inducements that might be offered for delay. On and on they went.

"Why are you so quiet, Daphne?" Anna asked.

"I'm thinking of my sister Lucy, a generation ago in the first World War and a man she met and loved right from the first moment."

"What?" Kevin said. "Tom?"

"Oh, no, no, a man from another part of the country. He was nothing like Tom."

"What's that got to do with this?"

Daphne didn't try to explain. In her mind's eye she saw the radiance that had surrounded Lucy for those brief weeks. When it all ended, a sort of melancholy had descended on Lucy's sweet face and it had never entirely lifted.

The room was quiet. It's up to me, Daphne thought, they're leaving it up to me.

"I'm going along with it all," Daphne said. "It's

Annie's life. Who are we to think we're such sources of wisdom?" She looked at Kevin. "Are we such fine examples of good decisions and happy marriages?"

There was now complete silence in the large room. No one rattled a drink or even audibly breathed.

Then Anna spoke. "Daphne's right. If I know Annie, she's going ahead with this marriage with or without us. We may as well try to make it a happy memory for her. Even a moment of happiness can never be lost, or taken away once one has had it." Her face was still and sad.

Through all the confidences she's heard from me, Daphne thought, she's never really opened her own heart. She, like myself, was a poor southern aristocrat. Her husband was so much older and more staid. Had she, too, paid a high price for her luxurious life? Perhaps she, like Lucy, had a brief but shining moment that she treasured for a lifetime. *And I don't even have that!*

On the very next day, Daphne began a brief episode that she would treasure for the rest of her life. She was able to get a seat on an airplane to Washington. There she met her Annie and they spent a glorious week in the Willard Hotel buying, buying, talking, talking, sharing the room and the hours with nothing but harmony between them.

At the end of that week they were joined by

Kevin, Anna and Bart. The Army airplane that was at the General's disposal arrived and they headed at top speed for the West Coast.

San Francisco lived up to Annie's expectations. General Young and his wife Amelia were an impressive, if formal, couple. The cordial Southerners provided enough warmth and ease for them all.

"That's what we Southerners are good for," Anna said to Daphne. "We oil the wheels of social concourse. Yankees and Midwesterners can scoff all they want to. They're glad enough to have us on hand in awkward situations."

The marriage took place in the chapel at the air base. Annie was breathtakingly beautiful in her white satin gown with Anna's lace and tulle veil floating around and behind her. Bartrum might have come straight from central casting in Hollywood, so handsome was he in his dress uniform. Daphne in soft blue could have been the bride's lovely older sister.

The bridal group left the chapel under the crossed swords of Bart's fellow officers. A small group of Bart's and the General's friends joined the party that followed at the Officers' Club. Kevin rose to the occasion and was an expansive host. Champagne, the finest scotch—things only Generals had access to—flowed freely.

When the bride and groom left for San Francisco, the parents continued the celebration. It ended on the proper note, with each praising the others' offspring and each assuring the others that all signs pointed to a happy union.

As it turned out, Annie and Bart had almost a year on the West Coast. First the Germans and then the Japanese surrendered. It was to take part in the Occupation of Japan that Bart finally departed.

* * *

Annie joined her parents in Louisville to wait until Bart returned to the States, thus setting the pattern of the future years. Whenever possible, Annie accompanied Bart wherever he was stationed. If wives were not allowed, she came home. But Daphne could tell this was no longer home for Annie. She had become a true Army wife. Home was any air base or any place where Bart was.

Daphne often felt inadequate during Annie's home visits. Annie was so self-assured, so confident.

"Really, mother, all these servants. What do you do with your time?"

"Annie, I can't imagine speaking to my mother like that. What *should* I do with my time?"

Annie was a pretty young woman, fair and blue-eyed, "But not so pretty as her mother." How many times had Annie heard that? She must not have liked hearing it. But Annie was clever and intelligent, too. All the love and attention may have spoiled her but it had made her confident—so confident, so satisfied.

Ah, Daphne thought, I'd rather have that than anything—to be, if only vicariously, confident and satisfied.

In time, two babies were added to the traveling household; first a boy, then two years later, a girl. And Daphne experienced what was possibly the purest happiness of her life—at last a moment of unadulterated joy—when she first held a grandchild.

But Mama's death, in 1947, came before these joyous events. Mama gone! Daphne was amazed at the depth of the grief and loss she felt. She'd been away from her family so many years. Why was she so bereft?

When the sisters were gathered at Ashton for Mama's funeral, Daphne felt the strongest pull not to leave them.

Oh, there's nothing like a sister. Why have I cared so much about all the little things, about Lucy loving Sally more than me, about Jenny being petted and indulged, about Lyda being so admired? Oh, help me, help me—was she praying? Was this a prayer? She didn't know, but inside her head it was echoing—help me to be content, at least content, for the time that remains to me.

Back in Louisville, Daphne began to think, to engage in true introspection for the first time in her life.

Anna was failing visibly, Anna, who after Mama and Papa had been the prop upon which she leaned.

What would she do without Mama and Anna? Now *she* must be a prop, a source of comfort and wisdom. But who needed her? Not self-sufficient Annie, not anyone.

On a spring afternoon, a year after Mama's death, Charles telephoned. "Miss Daphne, please come quick," he said, his voice breaking. "Susan just went in to check on Miss Anna 'cause she stayed in her room so long. She's gone, Miss Daphne, gone, just went in her sleep."

"Call Doctor Smith right now, Charles, I'll get hold of Mr. Kevin. I'll be there in a few minutes."

So they buried Anna, the best friend Daphne had ever had. Daphne was not surprised at her own grief, but Kevin seemed stricken. That did surprise her. She had thought him capable of only superficial emotions. To tell the truth, she hadn't thought about him much at all for a long, long time.

She considered him now—such an unexceptional man—middle-aged, middlingly endowed, spoiled, yes, spoiled by her beloved Anna. He had never had his feet held to the fire, no, never. Well, *she* had. Any child of Papa's had to measure up. She'd been the one to measure poorly, not intelligent enough, not noble enough, not strong enough. Well, Papa— she still had conversations in her head with Papa— let me just show you what I'm made of. I'm going to take this man I would have and make a life for what remains to us.

"That's the right thing to do, isn't it Papa?" She realized with a start that she had spoken aloud.

So she began to travel with Kevin. They went to Europe. This time Kevin took an interest in everything they saw.

Oh poor continent, I wish Papa could see this. What would he say about it all? The Holocaust, the great worldwide war, the atom bomb, the old cultures so devastated? Even Kevin agreed with her that Papa would have been able to make sense of it.

Back in Louisville she began to show an interest in the stables. At first she faked this interest but it became genuine. Everybody acts and talks like these racing people now, Daphne told herself. Why shouldn't I try to fit in? If Mama could manage to be interested in all that crazy stuff Papa was always carrying on about, I guess I can fit in with Kevin's friends if I set my mind to it.

The parties Daphne gave during Kentucky Derby week became quite renowned. Invitations were coveted items.

Oh, wouldn't Anna have been pleased with me? I wish I'd tried sooner. Well, better late than never. Was she at long last becoming confident in her abilities? Was old age to be her finest hour?

Daphne made an effort to visit Ashton at least once a year. Mary and Ned kept things running just as Mama and Papa would have wanted. They made all the sisters and nieces and nephews welcome so that they felt that it was still their home.

Her health was declining, as was Lyda's. Daphne could fly to Wilmington to see Lyda straight from her visit with Jenny in Columbia. Then she would rent a car to drive to Charleston to see Sally. She was easier with Sally now. She wished proud Sally would accept financial help. But that she would not do. Daphne saved Lucy for last, so that she could go home with that warm accepted feeling Lucy always generated.

Daphne and Kevin were always available to Annie and Bart and their children. Children needed roots, ancestors, blood kin. What did those Army people know about such things? She and Kevin provided stability for their grandchildren. It was the right thing to do.

After all, I have my triumph, my one real success—Annie.

My Annie is made of stern stuff. She's like Sally or Papa—like Sally. Why had she never noticed? She felt her spirits lift. To have her child be like Sally, strong, unbreakable—what a fine thing. What a triumph!

Sally

Charleston, 1948

WITH MR. FERGUSON'S HELP, Sally found a job almost as good as the one she was leaving. It was with the Rudyard, Allison law firm, and she would work for Mr. Rudyard himself. Liz and Benjamin urged her to live with them. The previous year Eloise had amazed them all by removing herself from Tradd Street to a retirement home that had recently been built in Summerville. It seemed that old Mrs. Carsworth had left the family mansion to Crawford's daughters, with Eloise to have its use for her lifetime. Liz had been overjoyed to move in and begin repairs and redecorating. Of course it would take years of work and far more money than they had right now, but what fun to get started. Liz's boys were at Porter-Gaud school, nearby. She and Benjamin loved the old sections. She had planned to make the third floor Ellie's separate apartment.

"Mother, thank you for coming. My boys are so happy. You'd think Mrs. Santa Claus was coming to town."

"I'll do my best to fill that role. I never plan to say 'no' in their presence."

"You can have the third floor, like when you were a bride."

But Sally stuck to her position. She'd been independent too long, she must have her own place. It was Thomas who found the perfect spot. One of the formerly fine homes on Savage Street had been made into four apartments. The owner lived in one herself. The unit that had been vacated was on the first floor, so the rooms were big with high ceilings. The back door opened onto a courtyard. No Charleston townhouse was without a sheltered garden area in the back.

She would need furniture. Her sisters fell with zest upon the task of seeing just who could spare what.

Sally was packing clothes and her few other belongings in Columbia one night when the phone rang, later than usual.

"Sally, it's Eloise calling from Summerville."

Sally was so shocked she had to sit down. She'd had a letter from Eloise when Ellie died, but no more.

"I've heard about your proposed move to Charleston. I think it's a very good idea."

Well, it had taken quite a while but she had finally managed to do something right!

"Mother left her furniture, silver, china, everything but the house itself, directly to me. It's all in storage. I have only a bedroom here so I just brought what was in my own room at home. I would be most pleased if you would take the rest. It's left to Liz's sons in my will. I'll have my lawyer draw up something, then you can leave it to the boys yourself."

Sally was hard put to believe that her hearing was functioning properly.

"Why Eloise, what a very generous offer. Let me think it over."

"Please don't waste our time thinking about it. I know I never showed it and I should have, but I've always admired you. Let me do this small thing to prove that you have not been entirely unappreciated by Crawford's family."

There was a long pause. Then, "Thank you, Eloise. Thank you for the kind offer, which I accept with pleasure, and thank you even more for the kind words and thoughts."

"That's settled, then. I'll send Benjamin the key to the storage vault and the letter from my lawyer. Goodbye, Sally." She hung up.

So Sally moved yet again, feeling the stirring of a hope that she prayed might lead to peace, if not exactly happiness.

Sally tried very hard to muster some of her old energy and enthusiasm.

I will not live in fear and anxiety. I will not become a person who's afraid. I will not break.

"I've made up my mind," she'd told Lucy. "I will *not* break."

Lucy had smiled. "Sally, if that mind of yours is made up, the rest of us can forget it."

"You're not so easy to dissuade yourself."

"I guess you're right. Stubbornness is a family trait. Comes in handy sometimes, too."

Sally loved her work. It was a blessing—well disguised at the time, but a blessing nonetheless—that she had to work. She couldn't imagine a life filled with teas, luncheons, and bridge games. Her old friends rallied around. She ate occasional dinners and luncheons with them. She was glad she could still make people laugh, relax, enjoy things more because of her presence. But she didn't want that for her real life. Next to Liz and her boys—yes, and Thomas, too—work was her life.

Her work, as she thought of it, was the *real* world. Mr. Rudyard advised bankers about how to avoid government interference. He helped his business clients buy companies, fight off big Yankee financiers who might wish to buy them. Sometimes he helped a friend keep a home that had been in the family for a hundred years or more and was in danger of being sold at auction for unpaid taxes. Sometimes he helped a woman, a woman who might have been herself a generation ago, gain some financial support and a separation or divorce from an impossible husband. She lost herself in these other people's lives. She went home to her own life, tired in body but refreshed in spirit.

* * *

She'd been in Charleston for a year when Thomas called one spring evening.

"Aunt Sally, I have here in my office an old friend of yours. Well, he's telling me to say he's an old admirer. Do you remember Mr. Colvin Withers from Atlanta?"

"Why of course I do, my wonderful boss at my very first job."

"He has a home at Yeaman's Hall now. He's retired and spends his winters there. We ran into each other on the golf course today. Your name came up and he remembers you—well, he's saying to tell you that it's more accurate to say that he's never forgotten you. May we drop by for a drink? I'll bring the drink, I know you never have any."

"Yes, do come on over. Tell Mr. Withers to bring his wife, too. He's surely married. Tell him I say so many Atlanta women were pursuing him, someone must have succeeded in the chase."

"His wife died two years ago. His son lives in Boston. He's telling me to say he's lonely, needs cheering up. Listen, this three-way conversation is driving me crazy. See you in thirty minutes or so."

Her spirits lifted. A man!

She fixed her hair, applied discreet makeup. Thank heavens her skin had held up, her best feature. She decided to change to a more becoming blouse. Her figure was still good—another thing to be grateful for.

The doorbell rang.

Yes, she recognized him. He'd held up pretty well himself, still trim, still had hair, the blond now so shot with gray that it was a sort of ash color. His face was still open, earnest, *nice*. His eyes lit up when he saw her.

It seemed he had a close Charleston friend from his University of Virginia days who had also been a realtor. This friend, Tom Phillips, had persuaded him to buy his Charleston home. He'd had it almost two years now, loved the club, Charleston, all of the friends he'd made.

"You know the Charlestonians all remind me of your Uncle Edwin," he said. "Mr. Edwin was like a father to me, since my own died young."

"I know he left you his part of the business, so you must have been like a son to him. I was so sad to hear of his death and then Cousin Roberta's. They were good to me when I needed it most."

She met his eyes. "You, too, Colvin."

He flushed, just as he had when he was younger, but he held her gaze until it was she who looked away.

Then Thomas intervened and they fell into easy chatter.

The next hour flew by. When she was seeing them to the door, he turned.

"I've loved getting reacquainted with you, Sally. Could I call you sometime? We could keep each other company for dinner."

Behind his back, Thomas winked at her.

"Yes, do call, Mr. Withers..."

"Oh please, over twenty years ago we established that you're to call me Colvin."

"Well, Colvin, I'd love to have dinner."

The telephone rang the very next day as soon as she had settled at her desk.

"Mr. Rudyard's office," Sally said.

"Sally, it's not Mr. Rudyard I want, it's you. How about dinner at the Yacht Club on Saturday. This is Colvin."

"Of course. I accept with pleasure—what time?"

"I'll pick you up at seven-thirty. How's that?"

"Fine, see you then."

* * *

Addie came on Saturdays. She was now a married woman with a husband employed at the Naval Base and with three children, all troublesome. But Addie, perhaps indoctrinated by Sally, marched to her own drummer. She was housekeeper for a Yankee family who owned a large house on the Battery. They were only in residence from December to mid-March, but she was on a retainer and went in regularly to be sure that things were shipshape when the owner and his wife did return.

She and Sally had kept in touch throughout the years. When Sally moved back, Addie said, "Miss Sally, I'll come over on Saturdays. You always liked your clothes just so—I'll do them up for you once a week. Maybe I can help with the house, too."

So she came every Saturday, kept Sally's clothes "just so," put a spit and polish on the few rooms and the two women had the considerable pleasure of each other's company.

Sally and Addie liked to reminisce about the years when Liz and Ellie were small. Addie seemed as proud as Sally about how well her girls had turned out.

"You should be," Sally said. "I could never have made it through those early years without you."

They didn't talk much about Ellie's death, just one good conversation during which they both cried. Then they closed that subject.

Mostly now Sally tried to advise Addie about her own children.

"Johnny's set on going to New York," Addie said. "Says Benedict College is no good. He wants to live with Joe—remember him? Mama's youngest brother? Well, Joe took himself up North in 1931. Did real well too, got an education, teaches sixth grade in some big, big school right in the city."

"Why, Addie, Johnny sounds like a young man with plenty of gumption to me. If Joe will take him in, maybe he can be a New Yorker and go free to CCNY. That's a fine school, I think."

"Well, my old Ralph's dead set against it."

"You've got to stand up to Ralph, Addie. Times are changing fast. Johnny needs to live somewhere else where he has more advantages and can get ahead of the game. He sounds mighty smart to me. You know Thomas and Benjamin will help him get to New York."

Addie never needed much encouragement when it came to standing up to people. So it came to pass that Johnny arrived in the great city.

"He's enough like you, Addie," Sally said, "that I'll bet on him making it all the way in and then out of CCNY."

On the Saturday following Colvin's call, Sally could hardly wait for Addie's arrival.

"Addie, guess what? I've got a date tonight, a Mr. Colvin Withers. I worked for him in Atlanta. He's a widower and has a house at Yeaman's Hall. Come help me decide what to wear. We're going to the Yacht Club for dinner."

Addie looked over the meager selection in Sally's closet.

"Miss Sally, them folks dress up on Saturday at the Yacht Club. These clothes won't do. Call Miss Liz and buy you something that's more right. Now do it, Miss Sally, right now."

Sally did. She and Liz combed King Street, came away with a coral "new-look" dress, wide skirted, clinched in waist, low neck. Sally didn't like the post-war long length at all, dreary looking—like the Depression clothes. Besides, she thought she was too small and she liked to show her pretty legs. But the low neck, that suited very well. Thank heavens her skin, all over, had held up.

She spent a long time getting ready. It felt good to look one's best. Poor Glen, she had not had enough energy to bother with him after Ellie died, although he tried very hard to be a comfort. Now Colvin was so much more interesting. He made her feel alive, young. Oh yes, there was nothing like a man for making a woman—well, a woman like Sally—feel good.

Over his first drink, which he sipped very slowly, Colvin looked across at Sally and said, "I'm so very sorry about your daughter. I've heard she was lovely and bright, like you, like Liz—I've met Liz, you know, but I didn't know she was yours."

"The girls looked like Crawford, they inherited his best characteristic."

"I'm so sorry about your husband, too. You've had a rough ride. But you don't show it." He paused, sipped his drink. When she looked up and met his eyes he said, "You're just the same. I can't believe you're so unchanged."

"Well, let's just say, my head is 'bloody but unbowed.'"

He looked at her steadily, his gaze intent.

"I'm sorry you lost your wife, I wish I'd known her."

"Thank you. You would have liked each other."

There was another pause that Sally felt no need to fill. Then he said, "I was very, very smitten with you back in Atlanta. I'm afraid I made a first-class fool of myself, trying not to show it but at the same time unable to stop myself from making it obvious."

She laughed. "You were a perfect gentleman but it was an impossible situation—you, my boss and me a married woman. Now I'll confess I tried hard not to like your liking me, but I did."

"Did you like me, too, just a little bit?"

"More than a little bit."

Once more his open face told her how pleased he was.

"Now, Colvin, that's enough about ourselves. Tell me about what happened to all those nice Abbott Company people, especially the typing pool."

So he began to fill her in on marriages, departures, the great changes in how things were done in his business.

"I loved it all, but it was time for a new generation to take over. My son, Colvin, Jr., is at Harvard Law School. Wants to practice up East. So I sold my business and here I am."

And here she was. Having fun—the first real fun she'd had since she could scarcely think when.

Friends came over to speak. Colvin was well-liked. Sally had not been forgotten.

Sally spent as much time as they could give her with the twins. What could be more fun than the company of maturing males? She was their chaperone of first choice. Then there was the work, the work. She hoped to work until she dropped. Proper Mr. Rudyard was the perfect boss. His appreciation of Sally seemed to know no bounds.

And Colvin—now that she was free to enjoy him, she could admit to herself just how appealing he was—intelligent, successful, but so modest and natural and unassuming. A rare sort of man.

Sally, unbroken, shone and sparkled.

* * *

When summer approached and the time for Yeaman's Hall to close drew near, Colvin telephoned, as he now did every few days.

"How about riding over to the Isle of Palms with me Saturday afternoon? We can have seafood for dinner. I want to show you something."

"I'd like that, Colvin. What time?"

"Is four too early? Dress comfortably."

What he had to show her was a beachfront house he'd bought.

"I think young Colvin would enjoy it here for vacations, don't you?"

"Of course he would. I'm sure he'll love the beach and there's no finer coastline in America than right here. I'll look forward to meeting him."

She knew that wasn't why he'd bought the house. Apparently Mr. Colvin Withers was going to leave no stone unturned in his pursuit of Sally Carsworth.

Well, she didn't want to discourage him. She was enjoying his company. She'd had enough misery and she was going to take any pleasure that came her way and not worry about the future.

She liked Colvin's son, though he was not much like his father. Still Sally was pleased to see that young Colvin seemed to like and approve of her.

"It's great to see Dad happy again," he said. "I want to thank you, Mrs. Carsworth, for being so kind to him."

"Well, he's not hard to be kind to. He's one of the nicest men in the United States of America."

Colvin's time in Atlanta became the visits; Charleston, his regular residence.

It had been more than a year since the telephone call from Thomas that had brought Colvin back into Sally's life. Next to Liz's family and Thomas', she saw more of Colvin than anyone else.

She declined all his entreaties to visit him in Atlanta or to accompany him on any of the trips he kept suggesting. He always made sure that she understood that other couples, proper chaperones, would be along. Dear Colvin, still trying not to embarrass her.

"Thank you for wanting me, but my job has to come first," she said. "When I get my brief vacations I need and want to see my family. You know how I feel about my sisters, especially Lucy."

"Lucy is absolutely lovely in every way. I think your relationship is wonderful. Couldn't she and Tom go with us to New York?"

"Colvin!" She laughed. He gave up with grace—always the gentleman.

Bless Colvin's heart, he held off as long as he could. It had been a full year of proper "dates."

One night after dinner, over brandy furnished by himself mainly for himself, Colvin began.

"Sally," his face was flushed. He *was* sweet, still so youthful in some sort of way.

"I've loved you since the first week you spent in my outer office back in the twenties. I had a good marriage—please don't think for a minute that I didn't—good wife, good son, success—so lucky. But other than that girl—of course the type pool girls informed you—the girl who ditched me almost at the altar—well, other than her, you were my strongest *passion*.

"I've got a second chance now. Won't you marry me, Sally?"

"Dear, dear Colvin. I wish you hadn't asked me. I don't think I can marry again ever. I've been through too much. I'm used up. I don't want any more strong emotions. I like things just as they are."

"Will you at least think about it? I want to take

care of you. Show you Europe, New York—give you a taste of leisure and luxury. You deserve it."

"Along with your charming self, that is very, very tempting. But I'm so used to living alone, pleasing no one but myself. Can we put it on the back burner?"

"Well, yes, if you insist, that's what we'll have to do."

He came over to the sofa where she sat and took her hand, kissed it.

"We're not too old, Sally, but we will be soon. Please think about it."

She did, but something in her held back. She hadn't broken but inside she was bent, yes, very bent. She no longer felt like stepping up to take the risks. She felt like hunkering down and enjoying any pleasant moment that came her way.

She told him so. He understood.

"All right, Sally, we'll hunker down. I'll take the pleasure of your company, anyway I can get it."

"Mother." Liz was so serious, all business, really not much like Sally had been at her age.

"Yes, darling?"

"Do you plan to marry Colvin?"

"I don't think so, Liz. Somehow I've been through too much—too much time with my back to the wall. I like to be alone. I like him very much, but no, I don't plan to marry him."

Liz never said if she approved or disapproved of her decision.

One night, again over a brandy in Sally's living room, Colvin said, "Sally, are you sure about not marrying? I love you. I want to spend what remains of my life with you."

"Oh, Colvin, I wish you wouldn't rock the boat. I like my life the way it is now. I can't tell you how much you add to the pleasure of my existence. But I want to be fair to you. Heaven knows how many women in this city or Atlanta or any city would jump at the chance to marry you. I ought to let you go, to find some wonderful woman who does want to get married."

"Do you really care for me?"

"Yes, I do. I expect it's love. I care a very great deal for you. But, as I said, I can't rock the boat of my emotional life. I've got to stay steady. I've survived but there's no bounce left in me. I can't risk another big emotional commitment. Colvin, dear Colvin, do you understand? Find another woman. I've taken up too much of your life. Find a younger woman. You've got so much to offer. I'm used up."

"No, I'm not going to do that and you know it. It's you or no one. I'll take your time and company on any terms. We'll keep on keeping on. Now what shall we do next Saturday?"

* * *

Two years later Colvin had a heart attack while playing golf at Yeaman's hall and died in the ambulance that was speeding toward Roper Hospital.

Sally was deeply saddened. Colvin had perhaps loved her more unselfishly than any of the men who had been attracted to her through the years. Yes, she could have granted his heart's desire and married him, but then the sadness would have been worse, much worse. She had had more than her quota of sadness.

"It was fine while it was fine," she said to Liz. "It's over. I live day-to-day now. What more do we have for sure than just the day, the moment, right at hand?"

Sally and Lucy

❦

Charleston, 1965

"Mother," Liz said, "you've got to see a doctor about that cough. You say you've quit smoking, and you have—*yours*. You're the greatest bummer I ever saw or heard of. Mother, please."

So she saw her doctor.

Numerous X-rays, consultations and office visits later, her doctor said, "Mrs. Carsworth, the tests confirm what I feared from the first. It's your lungs. It's malignant. There's no room for doubt."

Thomas insisted that they leave no stone unturned, she saw other doctors, but the bottom line remained the same. Lung cancer, too advanced for surgery. She could try radiation, the newest treatment. It *might* give her some extra time; it would certainly make her ill.

"No," Sally said. "Let's let nature take its course. I've had a good run for my money."

She worked as usual, she spent time with Liz. She joked and laughed with her big handsome grandsons. She did not break.

The time came, and fairly soon, when she had to give up her job and spend most of her days at home. Addie took a leave of absence from her rich Yankees and came every day to do whatever was necessary for Miss Sally. Then a day came when Sally felt ill, really ill. She couldn't get up. She pulled the sheet to her chin and lay still. Addie and Liz bustled around. Was this the end? Was she never to get out of bed again?

After a few days' rest she got up, put her clothes on, made up her face, fixed her hair. She was not going to let Liz down or the twins. So she was on the porch rocking, taking deep breaths, her old tried and true tranquilizer, when Tom Thornton's little Chevrolet pulled up just in front of her, an intent-looking Lucy at the wheel.

The sisters embraced.

"Now I know it's a crisis, for sure. You drove yourself."

Lucy laughed. "It's never too late to improve upon one's short suits. I've got a suitcase. I'll stay a few days."

Sally felt relief, oh such relief; she hadn't realized how much she was dreading becoming dependent on Liz. But Lucy and Addie, that was different.

When night was approaching, the sisters went

back on the porch. Charleston was coming into bloom, the air was soft, salty and humid as always, but not yet hot.

"Spring's a good time to die, Lucy. Winter is the worst."

Another relief, not to have to force cheerfulness, to pretend she wasn't dying, why couldn't everybody be like Lucy?

She answered herself, out loud. "Lucy, if everybody were like you, it would be too good a world. That wouldn't do at all. Just as Papa said, how would we know what we are made of if we had too easy a ride through life? I suppose he thought it proper that Abbotts and Willoughbys be put through fire and brimstone so we could show our breeding."

Lucy smiled. "Well, I guess you showed 'em all. Papa would have been so proud of your courage, your fighting spirit. You're the most like him, you know."

"I guess so. I always wanted to be like Mama but *you're* like her. I think that's why I pulled against Papa so hard. We were too much alike, bringing troubles on ourselves, gravitating toward battles."

The sisters rocked in silence for awhile, then Sally said, "Lucy, let's celebrate. Your Thomas brought me a bottle of sinfully expensive brandy. A small glass once in a while might help me postpone the morphine, he thinks. Go pour us some, use Mrs. Carsworth's best Waterford glasses. We'll live it up."

When Lucy came back with the glasses and dainty linen napkins as well, Sally was smoking a cigarette.

"Lucy, your eyes are as big as saucers. What on God's earth difference can it make now? Cigarettes have always been my favorite vice. Have one with me."

Sally knew Lucy hated smoking. She'd never even tried to learn how, and Tom had at last quit. But she managed to get a cigarette lit and took a companionable puff or two.

She sipped the brandy.

"It helps, doesn't it?" Sally said. "I know how you feel. Just like I would, if it were you."

"I don't know how I'm going to do without you, Lucy said. "I suppose it's unusual, a relationship like ours. When we're not together—and that's been most of our lives—I still feel supported just knowing you're here."

"That's how I feel, too. I guess it's simply love, the best kind there is. The "in-love" love is mostly passion, physical attraction. It's what I felt for Crawford. All that opposition made me more determined to have him. But when I no longer respected him, it was really over."

"Good heavens, Sally, and there you were sticking with him to the end, and you call me stubborn."

"It was the right thing to do. Papa said it best, the old know-it-all. The instinct to do what's right is born and bred in us."

The sisters rocked and sipped in silence for a while.

Then Lucy spoke, very softly.

"Of course, that's what I felt for Adam—passion, enormous physical attraction. But Sally, it was love, as well. I just never felt anything so overwhelming again, even my love for Thomas is a gentler thing."

There was another pause.

"Nowadays, of course, we would have slept together."

"Maybe that's the best way," Sally said, "to see how much is physical and what's left after that."

"I wish I had. Slept with him."

"Oh, Lucy, he would never have permitted himself to do it. He adored you."

Lucy signed, "You're right, of course. He's the one who wouldn't let us go beyond those kisses. I'd have done anything he wanted."

Sally laughed. "Who but you, Lucy, who else in the world but you would spend a lifetime faithful to a dream?"

"Well, it was a dream-come-true. Papa was right. That's a blessing given to only a few."

Thus they closed the subject, letting Papa's wisdom stand, as it had so often.

Sally went downhill fast.

Pale, panting, she finally surrendered and stayed in bed.

"Yes," Thomas said. "It's time for the morphine."

He arranged for a nurse, who came every morning. Addie took care of the house. Lucy never considered leaving. Tom brought her more clothes, spent several nights with Thomas, drove back and forth to Ellerton. Liz came every afternoon and sat with her mother while Lucy went for a walk.

"I'll go up Savage Street," she said, "and on to the Battery. This old city is bursting into bloom, its glory season. Walking is so calming. I love it, Sally—like you, like Papa."

Every day Sally grew weaker. Gaunt, frail, she gasped for breath, and reeked of death.

The sisters conspired to have Liz spared the worst of it. Sally rested, sipped what liquids she could manage, took her maximum dosage of morphine, let Lucy fix her face and hair, and composed herself for Liz's visits. When Liz went home, always saying as she left—"Call me, Aunt Lucy, call right away, if there's any sudden change."

"Of course I will," Lucy said. "Now, don't worry. We old girls enjoy being together."

Then Sally relaxed. She let the pain come, she rode it out. She did not break.

Lucy moved a cot into Sally's bedroom. The nights were bad now. She wanted to be close at hand. Sally hated to wake her. If she was close enough, she could know without being told when more morphine was needed.

On a very bad night, Lucy gave Sally double the usual dose. Thomas had said to do so if Sally asked for it.

The sisters lay quiet for a while. The soft spring air drifted through the open window. Lucy felt herself breathing in unison with Sally.

After a time, Sally spoke.

"Lucy, do you believe in God?"

There was a pause.

"Yes, I do. At least, I believe some benevolent force is guiding the destiny of this earth and its poor creatures. Nothing else makes any sense. How *could* we be born, not of our own volition, then strive and suffer and go into nothingness at the end? That idea is insupportable. Besides, Sally, at the worst times I've felt that force come in and sustain me. I know you have too."

"How else could I have survived?"

"I don't think Papa ever believed," Lucy said. "I suppose he was an agnostic—neither believing nor disbelieving, just open-minded. Remember how he used to make us stay inside during those fierce thunderstorms at Ashton? Then he would go out and pace back and forth on the porch, raising his face to the lightning and come in all exhilarated with the wonders of nature? He never talked about God. But we know Mama believed. That's how she was able to be so tranquil."

Sally didn't speak for a while, but she stirred, not sleeping yet.

Lucy said, "I know this much. Death couldn't possibly be a bad thing. It's the inevitable end to all life, and at worst it's simply peace. But you know it may—just may—be a wonderful thing, a great adventure, greater than any we've ever known. It's just like you, Sally, to beat me to it."

Sally managed a little laugh. "Do you think it might be true that in some way we'll be together with all the ones we've lost?"

Lucy paused a long while. "I don't know about believing exactly, but I hope. I could tell only you this, but I pray and hope that I may see Adam, just once again."

Sally managed another little laugh that became a sigh. "Oh, Lucy, Lucy. Of course, it's Ellie I want to be with."

"I think you will. I know you will, my brave Sally. You'll have the rewards you've earned in all your battles, the rewards for courage, for grace under pressure. You'll have Ellie. You'll have peace, perfect peace."

She got up and took Sally's hand. Then she stretched out on the hospital bed beside her, careful not to jar her failing, tender flesh, just touching her lightly, body to body, sister to sister.

"Mrs. Thornton! Mrs. Thornton! Well I'm just so sorry, Doctor. Your second visit today and here she is napping again. It's getting very hard to keep her alert."

The nurse's voice is loud enough to wake the dead. Still she keeps her eyes tightly closed.

"Never mind," Thomas says. "I'll come back soon. It was my father's death that changed her. It was a long and very devoted marriage."

She almost laughs aloud at this but she scrunches up her eyes instead and remains very still.

Poor Thomas—doesn't he realize that it was Sally's death that came close to finishing her?

Well, her marriage was long alright, and Tom was devoted. God knows she tried. She was faithful, dutiful, yes devoted too.

But deep inside her, beneath the toughening she cultivated, she has always felt an empty space—a space that could only be filled by someone else—someone brighter, quicker, more alive— someone whose touch was an electric shock, someone who could walk into a room and cause her heart and spirit to lift and sparkle.

She's satisfied that she stuck out the marriage with all the grace she could muster. She knows Tom did the best he could. If he had not been disappointed as well, he should have been—poor, dear Tom.

She remembers Tom's death—the cold morning that she awoke to find him dead beside her in Mama's old bed.

Well perhaps in a way Thomas is right and Tom's death had been the catalyst that truly changed her. She thinks of the winter day they buried Tom. She remembers that she felt relief— release. Yes. She remembers thinking—now, now,

I am released. I need no longer try so hard. Always I tried to do the right thing, feel the right thing. I shall quit trying. I shall please only myself. I shall think and remember. Now I can remember what I have tried so hard to forget. Now, yes—now—I shall make sense of it all.

* * *

"Well, Sweetie, what can I do for you?"

Who is it now? Is she never to be left in peace? It's some nurse she hasn't seen before. And "Sweetie!" Thomas has left strict instructions that she is to be addressed at all times as Mrs. Thornton.

She musters her Abbott-Willoughby voice.

"Why nothing at all, nurse. I am quite comfortable."

"Your light was on."

The nurse bustles over and punches the button to off.

"It was inadvertent. I'm very sorry to have bothered you. By the way, I am Mrs. Thornton."

The nurse departs.

Thank heavens. No rest in this place, 'no rest for the weary' Papa used to say—one of his little jokes.

Dear, Papa, you could not know just how weary the years could become. You didn't live that long. She longs for rest, to be left in peace. She's ready for that peace that passeth all understanding.

What night is this? Did Thomas—her proudest achievement, her life's work, her Thomas— did he come today?

Oh well, that's not important.

She can remember what she wants to remember—the privilege of age. She will think only of Him. She closes her eyes. She rests. She begins to feel as if she is floating—floating lightly, swiftly, higher and higher.

Ah, she sees His face, His face—the golden head above the crowd, the brilliant smile. She sees Him clearly. Moving closer, closer, bathed in glorious light.

Adam, my Adam.

* * *

"Good morning," says the bright-voiced morning nurse.

"Mrs. Thornton. Mrs. Thornton?"

The nurse hurries to push the bell.

"Come quickly, Mrs. Maxwell. I think we've lost Mrs. Thornton." She turns toward the head nurse, who enters at a trot. "Oh Mrs. Maxwell, just look at how Mrs. Thornton is smiling. One can see what a lovely girl she must have been."